My Brother's Lady, My Baby 1

Please Be Mine!

By

Sheena Perry

Sheena Perry
Publishing

Copyright

The *Tea* on the Author

Sheena Perry is originally from Dallas, TX. She was raised by her teenage single mother, Tonya. Sheena is the oldest of two children. Sheena's mother fell prey to the booming crack cocaine era of the 1980's. Entrusting a close relative with the task of babysitting her two kids, Tonya left for work one day not realizing that the family member would leave them alone and call DCFS.

At tender age of three, Sheena and her brother were removed from the home and placed into separate foster homes. While her brother was placed into a fairly nice foster home, she however suffered unimaginable abuse at the hands of her foster parents. She went days without eating, was fed dog food and she was tied to a chair throughout the day. Her thighs are still branded with the markings from the tight ropes.

Her mother was able to quickly regain custody of both children. However, later the same year she was molested by her mother's fiancé. Immediately reporting the abuse to her mother, the monster was quickly apprehended and served a lengthy stint in prison. Prison did not stop Sheena's molester from issuing out death threats.

He was heavily involved in the drug world and his threats were taken very seriously. Sheena's mom relocated her small family to Columbus, GA. After experiencing such traumatic events, she became extremely shy and withdrawn. She was even mute for two years. The once bubbly outgoing little girl had been replaced by an insecure, self-loathing shell of her former self.

As she became older, Sheena would contemplate suicide numerous times to cope with the unfortunate cards she had been dealt. She had even developed an eating disorder in her mid-teens. Sheena's mother continued to battle with her drug addiction throughout her childhood and into her young adulthood. Sheena has always had a deep passion for reading and writing. Reading has always been her outlet to escape the obstacles that she faced on a daily basis.

She enjoys romance, mystery, horror, autobiographies, thrillers and urban novels. From an early age, Sheena had tutored kids much older than herself. Sheena particularly enjoys writing short stories and poetry. She currently lives in Florissant, MO. Despite her rough beginnings, she was able to conquer all of her hurdles and meet many of her goals.

She was able to purchase her first house at the age of 20. A year later she gave birth to her daughter, Aaliyah. Somehow, she managed to overcome the murder of her daughter's father, who was killed by the police when their daughter was just 4 months old. She is a Registered Nurse. Sheena has a Master's degree in Nursing Education. She is currently in school pursing her Doctorate degree.

She works as a nursing professor at a major university and is the Director of Nursing at a long-term care facility. Sheena is also a licensed foster parent. Having had such a horrific experience during her time in foster care, she wanted to offer a safe home to children in need.

Please stay tuned for *Inevitable Deceptions: The Heart's Journey to Nowhere 3* which is Sheena's third and final installment of the series. She also co-wrote the children's book *I Made You From Scratch: You Are Perfect* with her daughter.

In addition to Inevitable Deceptions: *The Heart's Journey to Nowhere 3*, she is currently working on three other books: *The Whore Next Door: Welcome to Thotville, Do No Harm: License to Kill and Help! I Ate Peanuts, Now My Throat's*

Swelling Up! She has also published novels such as **The Girl Behind The Smile** by Dornisha Goodrich, **God Showed Me More Than Heaven** by K.S. Fisher and **The Living** by Frank Washington. Please stay tuned!

I attribute my success to this – I never gave or took any excuse. – Florence Nightingale

Connect with Sheena

Visit her website at www.sheenaperrypublishing.com

Friend her on Facebook at www.facebook.com/sheena.p.rn

Link with her on LinkedIn at
www.linkedin.com/in/sheena-perry-msn-rn-cne-22352486

Follow her on Twitter at www.twitter.com/sheenamperry

Follow her on Instagram at www.instagram.com/sheenamperry

You can also visit her business page at
https://m.facebook.com/SheenaPerryPublishing/

Submissions for all genres are now open. Please submit the first 3-4 chapters of your manuscript for publishing consideration. Allow up to 30 days for a response. Complete contact information including name, address, contact number and email. Use 12 pt. font, double-spaced in manuscript style format. Email manuscripts to submissions@sheenaperrypublishing.com.

We look forward to hearing from you!

Dedication

I'd like to dedicate this book to all of those who have been on the receiving end of abuse. Always know that it is never your fault. You are not alone. Don't be ashamed. Be your own advocate; seek help immediately before it is too late. Do not let your abuser have power over you. Remember that if they've abused you once, chances are that they will strike again.

In loving memory of Michael Calvin Perry, Doris Marie Green, Carolyn Marie White, James Green, Samuel Keita DeBoise, Erin LeighAnna Nabe, Lennette Berry, Michael Perry, Jr, Paul Anthony Sheets, Sr and Pauline Roberts-Perry.

I love and miss you all more than anyone will ever know. Rest in paradise.

~Sheena

Table of Contents

Acknowledgements

To my loving mother, Tonya Perry, I appreciate you for always being my biggest cheerleader. You have always inspired me to challenge myself. You are the strongest person that I know. I love you so much Ma!

To my brother, Rico, we may not always see eye to eye but know that I will always love you to the moon and back. No one can make me laugh the way that you do. You are my best friend.

To my beautiful daughter, Aaliyah, the day that I had you was by far the happiest day of my life. You made me grow up overnight. You are growing into the most amazing young woman that I could ever ask for. I know that your dad is smiling down at you from heaven. I hope that I have always been a positive role model for you and that you realize that you are my biggest motivator. All of my accomplishments were achieved with you in mind. Remember the sky is the limit and that the word *never* is not a part of our vocabulary. I love you baby girl.

To my friends and colleagues that have put up with my endless brainstorms and offered words of encouragement, I thank you for everything. I'd also like to thank my test readers who have given me constructive criticism.

I'd also like to give a special thanks to my readers who have purchased, downloaded and rated my books. You will never know how much your love and support mean to me.

Lastly, I'd like to thank the good Lord above. Thank you for continuing to bless me. Without you, none of this would be possible.

~Sheena

*****WARNING*****

THIS NOVEL CONTAINS STRONG LANGUAGE, BROKEN ENGLISH, SEX, VIOLENCE, AND VULGAR SITUATIONS WHICH MAY BE OFFENSIVE TO SOME READERS.

« Chapter 1 Martin And Pam »

"Kyle"

NOW BETWEEN YOU AND me, I fell in love with Julissa the moment I laid eyes on her. She was one of the most beautiful women…no scratch that. She was the *most* beautiful woman ever to grace this Earth. God had made her so flawlessly beautiful that she could've donated fragments of her beauty to fifty women and still been drop dead gorgeous.

I've always had a thing for petite women, and she was about as tiny as they came. Standing a mere four foot eleven inches, she bore curves that would make a coke bottle envious. Perhaps the most alluring thing about her is the fact that she was all natural. Aside from her signature cherry lip gloss, she always sported her face bare.

Her naturally curly hair always framed her delicate face perfectly. Her dimples gave her an innocent, yet sexy look like Debbi Morgan. Her pearly whites always appeared to gleam when she spoke. With her being an Airman, I always admired her discipline and the dedication she put towards her physical fitness.

Unfortunately, as much as I internally lusted over that amazingly beautiful species, she was off limits. For one thing, I had a woman, Amethyst. We called her Amy for short. She was beautiful too however; she knew it and felt the need to let everyone else know too.

Although she could easily live without all the pounds of makeup, she wouldn't be caught in public without her face being 'beaten to the Gods' as she frequently put it. Her hair and nails were done at least weekly...at my expense of course.

Being twenty-one, I didn't expect her to have her entire life mapped out, however, I sometimes wondered if she'd ever find her purpose. She jumped from job to job and went bat shit crazy at the mention of college. She was spoiled and self-entitled thanks to her parents. I was partly to blame too. We had been seeing each other for a year and instead of going back and forth with her, I usually just gave her her way in order to pacify her.

Amy was supermodel tall and was on the slim side. She was certainly no Julissa in the curves department. Prior to meeting Julissa, I had heard Amethyst talk to her over the phone on multiple occasions, but we had never met since she had been stationed in Iraq for the past year.

I had never really given her much thought until Amethyst decided to throw her a welcome home party. She also told my identical twin brother, Lyle that she thought he and Julissa would hit it off.

The plan was to link the pair up on the night of the party. Of course, as usual, Amethyst was going overboard on my dime for her friend's party. Hell, I didn't know why I couldn't treat the broad to Red Lobster and call it a day. The party's colors were purple, white and silver. We hired the hottest DJ in Boston just as my girl had requested. She was definitely going to be putting in some serious work in the bedroom for all this shit. I must admit, my girl was definitely a freak in the sheets!

Amethyst left the party to pick up Julissa at her father's house. Julissa didn't have a clue about the party that everyone had gone through the trouble of preparing for her. Whoever the bitch was, she better appreciate everything. I was down thirty-five hundred dollars for this party and felt some type of way about it.

Lyle arrived approximately twenty minutes after my girl left to pick up her friend. Being identical twins, Lyle and I were spitting images of one another. The few details that separated the two of us were the fact that I wore dreads, was tatted up and had a fanged grill. My brother on the other hand sported a clean-cut fade and was tat and grill free. Aside from those differences, it would be impossible to tell us apart. Growing up, our family couldn't even tell us apart.

That twin shit definitely had its advantages growing up. Me and Lyle were dark brown, six feet four inches tall and I can't speak for that nigga, but my third leg was ten inches long. We were some good-looking dudes, if I must say so myself.

"Damn bro, you went all out for Amy's little friend! You know she is trying to hook us up, but I haven't even seen a picture of her yet. She told me that she's on point, but she may be catfishing my ass. You know Amy hates my ass for real. I'm letting you know now; if Big Shirley waddles her big ass up in here, I'm out!!!" My crazy ass brother joked, but I knew he was dead serious.

"Naw bro, you know Amy doesn't keep ugly company. You have to be on point to kick it with her vain ass." I stated knowingly.

"Yo, Kyle that's what I don't get about you. Why are you with her shallow ass anyway? All she does is spend money and bitch. The pussy can't be that good my nigga!"

"See that's where you're wrong lil bro. Cuz that shit is GRRRRREAAAT!!!" I joked imitating Tony the Tiger.

"Those skinny bitches be taking the D for real man!" I continued once we stopped laughing.

Just as the DJ started playing Silk's Lose Control, Lyle tapped me on my shoulder.

"Yoooooo Kyle! There she is and she is bad as fuck!!! Look...look!!!" He exclaimed not attempting to hide his thirst.

"Aight nigga damn! Get off me!" I snapped smoothing down my expensive shirt.

You'd think his ass had never had pussy before by the way he was acting.

Slowly turning around, I wasn't expecting much. One thing that you have to understand about Lyle is that he was easily impressed by the most basic of bitches as long as their bodies were on point. His only hang up was big chicks. That boy definitely had a fat phobia.

My eyes first fixated on Amethyst. I couldn't help but notice how genuinely happy she looked in that moment. She really was a pretty girl. Then my eyes shifted to the mocha colored beauty standing to her left. My jaw literally hit the floor!

I wasn't the easily impressed type of guy, but she truly was a bad bitch! The crazy thing is, I could tell that her entire outfit cost less than a hundred bucks, however, she outshined all the other chicks who were wearing the latest designer gear.

As we slowly made our way over to the ladies, I was even more impressed by how much more attractive she was up close. Her skin was flawless! I watched as her eyes darted from both me and my brother. I guess she was trying to decide which one of us Amy was hooking her up with.

I couldn't help but feel a pang of jealousy as my brother annoyingly embraced her in a welcoming hug. That muthafucka was smiling like the cat that swallowed the canary. It literally took everything in me to refrain from clotheslining his black ass.

Once their pleasantries were exchanged, I decided to follow suit and hugged her as well. She smelled so amazing that I found myself holding onto her for a moment too long. The clearing of Amy's throat brought me back to reality.

"Girl don't be trying to rub up on all of this!" I joked to alleviate some of my embarrassment.

"Please, don't flatter yourself." She quipped.

For the remainder of the night I lurked in the shadows and watched Julissa. She appeared to be an extremely happy woman. Her smile was beautiful and her laughter was contagious. Eventually, I grew sick and tired of watching Lyle fawn all over her. I knew that I had no right to be upset, but somehow, I knew that she and I were meant to be together.

It was then that I knew that she and I would have a Pam and Martin type of relationship. It was the only way that I'd be able to hide my true feelings for her. I could tell my brother was feeling her already and I couldn't risk jeopardizing our relationship over a female again. Then again, she was no ordinary female...

« Chapter 2 Soldier Girl »

"Julissa"

IT WAS SO NICE BEING back home. I had graduated early and decided to join the Air Force when I was still seventeen. I come from a long line of Airmen so my dad, Julius, understood my desire to join and supported me whole-heartedly. Being an only child, my father never got the boy I'm sure every man wishes he had. I suppose I'm the next best thing. I've always been a bit on the rough side, a tomboy even. I'd take a game of basketball over Barbie any day.

I know my dad worried about me being a female in the military, especially after I was deployed, however, I could tell that he was also extremely proud of me. He bragged about me nonstop. He had retired after twenty-five years of honorable service himself. He had obtained several degrees in engineering during his military days, so he was able to jumpstart a secondary career as an engineer after his retirement from the military.

As proud of me as he was, I was equally proud of him. He had sacrificed a lot raising me. My mom had decided many years ago that she'd rather chase behind random men and drugs than be a wife and a mother. My dad chased right behind her trifling ass for years...mostly for me before he called it quits. I know it had to be difficult for him.

Luckily, we had a huge support system. Both sets of my grandparents were very active in my upbringing and so were my aunts and uncles. Perhaps my favorite aunt of all was Kandi, although I loved them all. Aunt Kandi was only twelve years older than me, so she was the one who babysat me the most. She was the one who taught me how to apply makeup, how to use pads, how to clean my "cookie", how to shave my legs and how to mend a broken heart.

As close as me and my father were, some things were reserved only for Aunt Kandi. I was born and raised in Brockton, Massachusetts. There's no better place in the world. Sure, it was cold as hell, but who cared?! I loved the diversity, the different cultures, the foods, the smells, and the men! New England men were by far the sexiest creatures on the planet. That is certainly not up for debate!

During my younger years, I do remember us moving a lot. While at the time I absolutely hated it, in hindsight, I have met some amazing people along the way. Many of which I am still acquainted with via social media. Things were rocky for a while until my dad stopped chasing after my mama. Once he directed his energy towards more positive avenues, positive things quickly began to happen.

My dad had a few girlfriends here and there that he'd introduce me to from time to time, but none of them were good enough for him in my book. Not even my own mama deserved him. I was always respectful to each one of them because he'd taught me to be a respectful young woman. I was definitely a daddy's girl. He was fairly strict on me when it came to dating and boys in general. I didn't even have my first boyfriend until after I had moved out and joined the military.

As everyone knows, Air Force training isn't for the weak despite people referring to us as the "Chair Force". Our basic training will have grown men on their hands and knees begging the Lord for mercy.

As crazy as it sounds, I loved every single second of that experience. For the first time in my life, I truly felt a sense of belonging. It was as if I was created for the Air Force. Listening to the other recruits' whine and cry baffled the hell out of me.

Yes, we never seemed to have enough food or time to eat. Yes, I couldn't think of many days in which I was permitted to sleep more than four hours. Yes, my hair was a nappy ass mess. Yes, I felt filthy even after my two-minute showers. Yes, I missed my family, freedom and social media. Being a female recruit was a rarity and I was the diamond in the rough who had made it to the other side.

The training actually came with a few perks. One, my body was pushed to such extremes that I didn't have a period for over four months. Two, my body had never looked better. As much as I looked forward to our boot camp ending, I was kind of sad when it did. It was a once in a lifetime opportunity and I was happy to have had the honor of experiencing it.

I had scored high enough on my Armed Services Vocational Aptitude Battery (ASVAB) test that I could have had any job that I wanted in the Air Force. I've always loved planes and wanted to select something that I could do on the outside of the military, so I opted to be a pilot. The training was very lengthy, rightfully so.

Fast forward four years later, here I was one of the best female pilots...scratch that. I was one of the best pilots around. I had just completed my contract and was taking a brief break prior to reenlisting. With my pilot experience, I was being offered a nice reenlistment bonus. How could I say no to that?!

I had been friends with Amy since middle school. I loved my home girl, but she was spoiled as hell. She never really had to work hard for anything. For as long as I could remember she had told me that she was going to marry rich, have babies and be a stay at home mom. She never really wanted more than that for herself. She was gorgeous with the build of a model.

I wished that she realized that she was more than a pretty face. She could do anything she set her mind on. She actually attempted to join the Air Force with me. However, she never made it past the physical at the Military Entrance Processing Station.

She was disqualified for her elevated heart rate; flat feet and home girl couldn't do the duck walk to save her life. Although she didn't make the cut and she wasn't able to swear in with me, she stuck around with my dad and watched me get sworn in.

She was an amazing friend and I loved her like a true sister. I guess that's why the circumstances surrounding the sexy Carlton twins made things so complicated. Amy and I talked as much as we could considering the circumstances. Once I got deployed, I have to admit I became homesick after a while and she did her best to make me forget about how alone I was. While I had made lots of friendships and bonds with my fellow soldiers, it just wasn't the same.

I always looked forward to her phone calls and letters. Me and my first boyfriend, Xavier, had split after he decided that he did not want to wait for me while I was deployed. He was against me joining the military in the first place, but it was always my dream. It was something that I had to do. We both knew that I would have resented him if I didn't follow my dream. I knew it was hard for him and I honestly commended him for at least trying and for also knowing his limits.

Once I received my deployment orders, I knew it was the beginning of the end for us. Telling him that I was leaving for nearly a year was the hardest thing I had ever had to do. I loved him more than I loved myself.

I had given myself to that boy. Unfortunately, I loved my career just a little bit more. It wasn't like I had the option to refuse my deployment one way or the other. My fate had been sealed for me whether either of us liked it or not.

I flew over to Afghanistan with a heavy heart. I was already sad about leaving my friends and family, but now I had lost the love of my life. Being a woman in a male dominated field, there was no shortage of suitors, but I wasn't interested in dating any of the men I worked alongside.

Not only was it against the rules to have sexual relationships, but I was just hyperfocused on the bottom line. That bottom line was staying alive and my career. The last thing I needed was to get caught up as some female soldiers tended to do.

Upon finishing my tour, I couldn't wait to see my family and Amy. Although I was exhausted from the long commute, Amethyst insisted that I hung out with her. Being the spoiled brat that she was, I finally caved.

When I entered that fancy hall, I couldn't believe that she had gone through all of the trouble on my behalf. I wasn't expecting anything that grand at all. I certainly felt special that night. It wasn't until we arrived that she told me that she was hooking me up with her boyfriend's identical twin brother.

I had never met either of them. While I appreciated the gesture, I still didn't feel prepared to jump back into the dating scene. Plus, Xavier still ruled a huge part of my heart. I wasn't fully prepared to let him go.

I was prepared to tell Amy as much, that is until we walked up to two of the sexiest men my deprived ass had seen in a long time. They were both a deep chocolate brown. They both towered over my slight frame. Hell, I was only one inch taller than the minimum height required to join the military.

I wasn't wearing any panties, so I felt myself leaking down my inner thighs by just the sight of them. One of the guys sported neatly styled dreads while the other one sported a fresh fade. The one with the dreads also had a well-kempt beard and his chiseled arms were covered in various tattoos. They were both dressed nicely without being overly flashy. The guy who sported the fade greeted me with a hug first. I politely welcomed the embrace.

The twin with the dreads came in for a hug second. Damn he smelled so good! Well they both did, but his scent was like an aphrodisiac imprinting on my soul. He was sending off pheromones that my neglected kitty just couldn't handle. As he bent down to hug me, I was literally being jabbed in my chest by his third leg.

I also noticed that he didn't seem to ever want to let me go. Hell, I didn't want him to either. I knew he had to be my man. I owed Amy big time for this shit! I guess he finally realized that he was hugging me a little too long, so he let me go after my girl cleared her cock blocking ass throat.

As he released me, he said, "Girl don't be trying to rub up

on all of this."

Of course, my smart ass told him not to flatter himself.

This led to all four of us laughing. It was then that my heart stopped. His grill was so alluringly sexy that I couldn't stop staring with my mouth open.

How could anyone be so damn perfect?!

At some point Amy cleared her throat once again disturbing me from my naughty thoughts.

"Hey guys, I want you two to meet my best friend, my sister from another mister...Julissa. Julissa, I'd like for you to meet Lyle Carlton. He's the one I told you about." She stated gesturing towards the twin with the fade.

She then continued, "And this is *my* man Kyle Carlton."

With that she draped her right arm around his neck. Damn! A momentary wave of disappointment washed over me before I said, "Hello Lyle and Kyle. I am very pleased to meet the two of you."

After we all exchanged pleasantries, Lyle swept me away so that we could get to know one another better. We ended up having a great time and at some point, I realized that I was happy that we'd met. Call me crazy, but every time I looked in Kyle's direction, his eyes were boring into me. One thing was perfectly clear; I was definitely going to keep my distance from him. He was dangerous...my "cookie" told me so.

« Chapter 3 Don't Ask, Don't Tell »

"Lyle"

I HAD LEARNED YEARS ago that one of the most profitable, yet legal hustles is the real estate game. I had been blessed to have stumbled upon the world of real estate. Just like any other investor, I had experienced my fair share of losses, but luckily for me, the gains by far superseded those losses.

For the most part I preferred flipping houses. I had a few rental properties, but I enjoyed seeing fast returns. Having tenants usually came with their own set of headaches.

I was twenty-two years old and living my best life. I had a two-year-old son named Jackson who I loved with every fiber of my being. His mother on the other hand was a different story. She used Jackson as a paycheck. Nothing was ever good enough for her.

She felt that now that she'd had my baby, she no longer needed to work. She thought that I should accommodate her by funding her lifestyle. Although I'd like to say that meeting Kamisha was my biggest regret, I knew that without her funky ass there would be no Jackson. He was the best thing to ever happen to me.

Although Kamisha and I were never technically in a real relationship, I was still excited when she told me that she was expecting my son. I never questioned his paternity or anything and at this point a test couldn't change how I felt about him one way or the other. Kamisha's scandalous ass later confessed to tampering with the condoms by poking holes in them during an argument. We'd never had unprotected sex so that made perfect sense.

It wasn't until after she became pregnant that her true colors were revealed. I couldn't believe that I had allowed myself to become eternally connected to such trash. I wouldn't wish a baby mother like Kamisha on my worst enemy. I paid her twenty-five hundred dollars a month for my son, yet she claimed that wasn't enough to properly care for him.

I also carried him on my insurance so that he wasn't on Medicaid. I was at my wits end with that broad. I had requested full custody on several occasions since she constantly bitched about her inability to care for him. But of course, she wasn't going to give up her cash cow.

As much as I wanted to just take her trifling ass to court, I didn't want to hurt Jackson. Although I hated everything she stood for, my son loved her crazy ass to death. I'd never want to deprive him of having her in his life.

I wasn't on papers or being forced to pay her child

support. I paid the twenty-five hundred dollars willingly. Sure, I could have gotten the courts involved and paid her a few hundred dollars a month, but I wasn't on any petty shit.

Kamisha wasn't a complete dummy. That's why she never took me to court. She knew most of my work was done under the table and in other names so on paper, I looked pretty damn broke. Sadly, some people were impossible to please.

Aside from my son's birth, meeting Julissa was one of the best events of my life. After meeting her, I reimbursed my brother the full amount that he'd paid for her welcome home party. She was so different from any other woman I had ever met. She was only twenty-one, yet she was so focused, ambitious and mature.

Her drive turned me on like no other. She was like a breath of fresh air. It was refreshing listening to her talk about her goals. She was the very first female I had come across who wasn't looking for a sponsor. It was a welcomed change from the typical blood sucking leeches out there.

Since meeting her at her welcome home party, she and I had been virtually inseparable. I had learned that she was raised by her dad, Julius. She was an only child, yet she was as giving and humble as they came. When I found out that she was a pilot in the Air Force, I instantly fell in love with her.

It's funny how her small stature made me want to protect her from the world, yet it was everyone else who needed the protection. I won't lie, I was not feeling her reenlisting, however, I would never make the same mistake that her ex had and allow her to slip away.

I feared that she would be deployed again and that she would be killed in the line of duty. I was just meeting her and didn't want to lose her already. I don't know why, but I never told Julissa about Jackson.

She never asked if I had any children and I subconsciously failed to volunteer that bit of information. I suppose I was afraid of chasing her off especially with a baby mama like Kamisha lurking around.

Don't get me wrong, I was not ashamed of my son. Not at all. Julissa didn't seem like the type to want to be bothered by a guy with a child...let alone one who also had a gold-digging baby mama.

I was stuck in between a rock and a hard place. I know you may be thinking I'm a cowardly fool and you'd be right. I should've just been up front and honest and if Julissa bailed then she wasn't meant for me anyway. The fear of losing her, however, was just that strong.

We have been going steady for a little over six months now and I was completely enamored with her. We didn't get to spend as much time together as we both would have liked, but when we were together it was as if we were never apart.

Our time away from one another made our time together than much better. She wasn't clingy and overbearing like a lot of the women I'd dated. Julissa actually gave me breathing room and the opportunity to actually miss her fine ass.

I could certainly see a future with her. She was the woman of my dreams. We weren't even having sex yet, but I was already her forever man. Glancing at the photo of the two of us sitting on my desk, I rubbed my chin. I tried to come up with a way to tell her about Jackson without losing her. Was it too late?

Would she actually leave me over a matter that had never come up? One thing was certain...I had to hurry up and tie Julissa down. Trap her even. I knew a proposal was in our near future. If we were sexing, you better believe that I would've already put a baby in her to keep her tied down. I'd die before I allowed her to leave me.

« Chapter 4 I'm Not Crazy »

"Amethyst"

DON'T BELIEVE EVERYTHING that you hear. Despite everything that people assume about me, my life isn't all peaches and cream. I was fortunate enough to be raised with both of my parents under one roof, however, that isn't always necessarily a good thing. Had my parents decided not to stick it out for us kids, we probably would've been better off. I'm not sure if my parents collectively equated to one half-assed parent.

My mom and dad were legally married and together they had four of us. I was the oldest and dreaded every second of it. My mom was one of those fat lazy ass people who was always looking for the next come up. She was the scheme queen. I don't think she'd ever worked a day in her life. Not honest work anyway. I cannot tell you how many times she's exaggerated her injuries from car accidents just to receive her guaranteed trips to the chiropractor and paycheck.

She was receiving social security checks for all of us growing up. I still get embarrassed thinking about all the crazy shit she had us telling those psychiatrists.

"Okay Amethyst don't go in there fucking this shit up. Tell Dr. Qayum that you have been hearing voices. And if she asks what they say to you, tell her nosy ass that they be telling you to kill yourself and other people, too.

Fuck it, tell her you be seeing weird shit too. I'm gonna tell her that sometimes I wake up to you standing over me in a trance holding a knife. Our stories have to match girl. We need this money. You've got to earn your keep. Shit ain't free." She coached.

We did the same song and dance every fucking time I had a psychiatry appointment. I don't know why she felt the need to tell me the same shit every time. I had that humiliating dialogue commenced to my memory.

I could still see Dr. Qayum's trusting eyes widen in surprise at the fabricated foolishness I was forced to tell her. She ate that shit up and mama's bank account thanked her. Mama would have me intentionally failing important tests at school to prove my "inability" to focus.

I was instructed to draw disturbing pictures of mutilated bodies in art class so that she'd be called up to the school. She would obtain the drawings to show at my next psychiatry appointment. I was forced to take bullshit medications that I didn't need.

They made me so sleepy that I was damn near robotic. It wasn't until I was older that I realized that I was not crazy. I had been exposed to counselors and psychiatrists for so long that at some point I had begun to believe the hype.

My poor sister and brothers had to endure the same bullshit for the sake of her beloved SSI checks. I hated her for that. My dad stayed so drunk that I don't think that he noticed much of anything happening around him.

Hell, he was on disability for his epilepsy, so my mom was definitely rolling in the dough. I'm not one hundred percent sure, but I'd once heard that she was receiving close to one-thousand dollars in food stamps a month.

During tax season she sold all of our information to the highest bidder. We were on section 8 and received assistance from virtually all outside resources dumb enough to fall for her charm. Did my siblings and I ever have to wonder where our next meal was coming from?

No, we always had a kitchen full of food. My mama always made sure that we were dressed in the latest fashion as well, but it all came with a price. She didn't dress us nicely because she was such a wonderful parent; she only wanted to keep up with the Joneses.

She kept us up to par because she used us as a badge of success. When we looked good, she looked good. She drove around in the best cars and we wanted for very little in the way of material things. It was instilled in me at a very early age that I didn't have to work hard. I was taught that I could cheat and abuse the system and still live in luxury. As I grew older, I realized that I had one up on my mother...my beauty.

I had always been conscious of my weight because I feared growing up and looking like my mother. I'd been afflicted with an eating disorder for as long as I could remember. While I had inherited her tall stature...that bitch could keep her rotund waistline. I was cool on that. I thanked the stars above that I took after my dad in the looks department. He was Mexican and black, however, he looked purely Mexican.

He was a very handsome man before alcohol took over and aged him before his time. His dark curly hair was typically kept in a long ponytail. Both of our skin was the color of toffee and our thick eyebrows were identical, although I kept mine thinly arched. He wasn't a big guy, but he did have a big heart during his rare sober moments. He pretty much went with whatever my mama wanted.

Now that I was an adult, I still received my monthly social security checks. While it wasn't a lot, it helped support me and I was able to take care of my basic needs. Anything beyond that, I relied on Kyle to take care of.

I was so pretty that men begged to take care of and support me. He was a little different from the other men I'd dated. He wasn't as giving and questioned the amount of money that I spent a lot. It could be frustrating, but I genuinely loved him.

When I looked at Kyle, I didn't just see dollar signs, I saw a future. My future. I eventually wanted to become Mrs. Carlton. We got along well for the most part, but I hated when he pressed me about finding a job or going back to school.

I didn't understand the purpose of any of that when he was perfectly capable of supporting the both of us. He made more than enough money with Lyle. He was a little bit on the cheap side and could be living so much better than he did.

After a year and a half of dating, I was hopeful that he was going to propose to me any day now. I was smart, beautiful, funny and was a huge freak in the bedroom. I could make his toes curl by just sucking on his ear lobes. I wasn't much of a cook or a housekeeper, but hell, we could hire a cook and a housekeeper. Why would he want his beautiful wife stuck in the house cooking and cleaning anyway when I could be shopping or vacationing?

Envisioning our perfect life together made my heart do somersaults. I wanted a huge family like my mama. I think four or five kids would do. We'd have to hire a nanny of course to help me, especially throughout the night. No man wanted a trophy wife with huge bags under her eyes.

"Hello, ma'am. How may I assist you today?"

Handing the woman a picture that I'd cut out of a magazine I replied, "Ahh yes, I suspect that my boyfriend will be proposing to me soon. I want to jumpstart my search for my wedding dress. Do you have anything similar to this?"

"Hmmmmm. Yes, I have something I think you'll love. Right this way dear." She responded.

« Chapter 5 There's Always A Dylan »

"Julissa"

"HEY HANDSOME! I figured you were hungry and brought you over some lunch." I stated to Lyle while bending down to kiss his full lips.

"Ummm ummmph ummmmph! Damn baby you taste so good! Just like cherries." He complimented while licking my remnants off his lips.

He was a great kisser and that sometimes made it difficult for me to refrain from jumping his bones.

After my first failed relationship with Xavier, I wasn't in a rush to completely give myself to a man just yet. I really liked

Lyle and could see a future with him, but I just wanted to be cautious. So far, he had been respecting my wishes.

Setting the homemade lasagna and garlic bread down in front of him on his desk, I walked behind him and began to give him a massage. He was always so tense, so I constantly greeted him with one of my infamous massages.

"Ummm baby! You never cease to amaze me. I've missed you so much. Come here woman." He responded turning around in his office chair.

His strong arms engulfed my small frame as he embraced me in a long hug. I absolutely melted. I felt myself turn into mush as I became intoxicated by his delicious scent.

The stirring of my kitty snapped me out of my lustful trance and had me pushing Lyle away.

"I'm sorry." I said wringing my hands together.

I was always so self-assured and confident, but Lyle always made me lose all control.

I had reenlisted into the Air Force two months ago, but I was fortunate enough to be able to be stationed near home. Now that I had reenlisted and climbed up in rank, I was permitted to live off base. I was so excited about that. I now felt a greater sense of freedom.

I was living on my own for the first time ever. I was actually renting out a small home from Lyle. While he insisted that I lived there for free, I insisted on paying him. My basic allowance for housing was more than enough to cover the rent, my utilities and my cellphone bill. I know Lyle was charging me much less than what the house was worth, but my man was stubborn.

I had been spending much of my time nesting and decorating my home. I never invited Lyle over out of fear that we'd lack the willpower needed to refrain from having sex, but I did want him to see what I had done with the place.

"Baby, what do you think about me throwing a small BBQ this Saturday? I want you all to finally see what I've done with the place. It's really coming along. Do you have any plans?" I inquired.

At first, he seemed to be in deep thought. He finally responded, "I can change my plans boo. I'd love to see what you've done with the place. I'll even be the one on the grill." He offered.

I jumped up and squealed with excitement.

When Saturday rolled around, I was so anxious about how my little gathering would turn out. I hoped everyone liked what I had done with my home. I know I was probably being a little extra, but I'd never had a place that was all mine. Living on base was similar to living in a college dorm.

I had found a lot of my décor at Target, Macys, and on Amazon. I had invited some of my military family, blood relatives, and of course a few friends. The house itself wasn't all that big, but luckily the back yard was huge. Lyle had it landscaped to perfection. I really loved it. It was my small paradise. I made my rounds playing the perfect hostess to all of my guests. They all told me how proud they were of me.

Even my Aunt Kandi was able to make it out which made my day. My dad and grandparents came for a couple of hours, but couldn't stay for the entire gathering. Amy and Kyle were also in attendance and had contributed a lot to setting things up. Kyle was manning the second grill with his brother.

"Damn Lissa, my brother lets you run around looking like a Chia Pet? When are you gonna run a hot comb through that birds' nest?!" Kyle's annoying ass said walking past me with a pan of ribs.

He was always taking shots at my natural hair. I wasn't a fan of perms or weaves. I loved the naturally curly hair that God had blessed me with.

I punched him in his arm causing him to nearly drop the pan of food.

"Shit! You hit like a grown ass man. Lyle man, you better hurry up and check your girl's drawls to make sure she isn't hiding a dick under that skirt!" He teased getting on my nerves.

"Amy, why did you bring K's ghetto ass here? I cannot stand his rude ass. He is forever talking shit!" I vented rolling my eyes at a laughing Kyle.

"Aye bro, leave my baby alone. I can assure you that she is all woman over here." He boasted while hugging me from behind. His lips soon fell to my neck and I let out a low moan.

My eyes never left Kyle's and I could see that a strange expression had taken over his face. He looked upset for a moment, but then quickly rebutted, "Nigga you can't assure me of shit when you haven't even smelled the pussy yet. I'm telling you, Lissa is hiding a big set of balls under that skirt!" He sneered.

I was about to respond but Lyle turned me towards him and covered my mouth with his, instantly pacifying me. I knew he was trying to calm me down so that I wasn't upset at my own party.

After a while I made me a large plate and sat down next to my Aunt Kandi and Amy. We laughed and joked about random stuff until Amy announced that she had to pick up a dress. I asked her why she couldn't just pick it up the next day and hangout a little while longer. She told me that she had been waiting for the dress for way too long and was anxious to finally try it on.

Throwing my hands up in surrender, I hugged my bestie and told her to call me once she made it home. Aunt Kandi and I watched her walk away and I couldn't help but to take in Amy's beauty.

Finally clearing her throat my aunt asked me, "Do you need to tell me something niece? You were staring at ole' girls' ass and shit for forever."

"Auntie, I was not looking at her ass...just at her. I hope that she finds her happy place. She's been through a lot and I worry about her, that's all."

"I don't know JuJu. She seems sketchy as hell. You know I've never really liked her little sneaky ass. Besides, her man is in love with you." Aunt Kandi stated seriously.

"Wha...what??? Auntie, no more alcohol for you tonight!" I told her.

"Now your Auntie Kandi may be a tad bit inebriated, however, I know what I know darling. Kyle wants you." She slurred.

"Auntie, Kyle and I hate each other. That man wouldn't piss on me if I were on fire." I retorted.

"Julissa, do you remember little Dylan from the first grade?"

I had to think back for a few moments and then I nodded my head.

"Do you remember how he put gum in your hair, put a frog in your book bag and constantly called you names?" She asked.

I again nodded. I definitely remembered that little terror.

"Well dear, Kyle is your new Dylan. Little Dylan eventually came clean and told us that the reason why he was so mean to you was because he loved you and that you were 'precious'. Just like Dylan, Kyle acts that way to deflect how he truly feels about you. He doesn't want Amethyst's ass, that's for sure. Stay away from them both niece." She warned.

"Oh auntie, come here so that I can take you to my spare bedroom. You aren't going anywhere like this tonight." I told her drunk ass.

Before standing up to escort my intoxicated aunt to her temporary room, I glanced up and saw Kyle's eyes fixated on me.

I blushed and quickly looked away. Shifting in my seat, I blocked him out and continued on my mission to get my aunt situated for the night. Kyle couldn't be feeling me, could he???

« Chapter 6 Imperfectly Perfect »

"Kyle"

TRUTHFULLY MY BROTHER and I rarely fought growing up which is hard for some to believe. Having to share damn near everything from a placenta onward...you'd think that we beefed constantly. No, it was none of that. We brothers embraced our likeness and closeness.

Our bond was unlike anything. It was something I wouldn't trade for the world. With that being said, watching Lyle all hugged up on Lissa made me want to put the boy in the hospital. I wanted to whoop his black ass for flaunting his relationship with her in front of me like that.

It was one thing for me to constantly be reminded that she was with him verbally, but to see the shit firsthand hurt like a muthafucka. I knew she hadn't given him any pussy yet, so I knew there was still a chance for the two of us. But how would we pull it off. How could she and I be together without hurting Amy and Lyle?

I hated lusting over and loving my brother's girlfriend this way. I had tried everything in my power to dislike her, but she was simply just too dope. I adored her imperfectly perfect ass from her nappy ass hair down to her calloused ass feet. While in her presence, there was rarely a moment that went by that I wasn't admiring her from afar. I always jumped at the chance to be near her.

My lovesick ass even volunteered to stay behind to help clean up. Of course, my brother got called away as usual. So, it was just me and Julissa left behind to straighten up her house. I didn't mind at all. I didn't have anything planned anyway.

Amy's ass had mentioned something about picking up a new dress or something, so I wasn't expecting to see her shopping ass anymore today. It took the two of us the better part of two hours to finally restore her house to its former glory.

She finally plopped down exhaustedly into a chair at her kitchen table. Seeing how weary she was, I walked up behind her and began to massage her tense shoulders. She initially stiffened under my touch, but eventually relaxed after I assured her that it was just an innocent massage. It wasn't long before I heard low feminine moans escaping from her pretty mouth.

The vibration of her phone caused her to stand and retrieve it from the island. I was rocked up and hiding it behind the chair. After she read the message, she looked at me and I couldn't help but to notice that her nipples rivaled my dick in the hardness category. She noticed my gaze and immediately crossed her arms over her small, but succulent chest,

"Ummmm, K thanks for helping out today. I really do appreciate everything you've done. Feel free to take some plates with you. I'm tired so I'm about to wash today off of me and hit the sack." She said.

I smiled and replied, "No thanks needed. I was glad to help. Maybe now you will have time to soak those corns and do something with that head of yours."

She sucked her teeth and rolled her eyes at me before saying, "Goodnight ya ignorant bastard. Lock up behind yourself."

With that she stormed off in the direction of her bedroom. Her little booty was jiggling from her angry steps and I was loving the show. I knew I needed to leave, but something in me wouldn't allow me to. I heard the shower in her bedroom bathroom turn on and I slowly followed her sweet scent in that direction. I slowly opened her bedroom door praying that Lissa didn't catch me being creepy.

I noticed the clothes that she'd worn today lying in a pile outside of the bathroom door. I know many of you are about to judge the fuck out of me for my next action but fuck it! Ask my dick if he cares?! I sifted through the pile until I ran across some sexy pink lacy panties. My dick rocked up even more just from me thinking about how she looked in them. That pink against her chocolate skin I'm sure was a deadly combination.

With my newly acquired panties in tow, I walked over to the bathroom door. Luckily, it was slightly ajar. I peeked in and almost lost it as I witnessed a naked Lissa inspecting her beautiful body in a full-length mirror.

She rarely dressed skimpily and preferred comfortable clothing, so it was rare to see her curves. She had the tiniest waist that led to a nice plump ass. Who would've guessed that she was hiding all of that under her military uniform?

Instead of getting in the shower, Lissa began pinching her nipples. I couldn't believe my eyes! That was my cue to release my anaconda. After pulling my dick out, I brought her panties up to my nose and inhaled her essence as I stroked my meat.

If only she knew that she didn't have to please herself that way. I would've gladly done it for her. Soon her hands went in between her juicy thighs and her sultry moans soon filled the small bathroom.

I had the perfect view of her ass and her pussy was visible to me in the mirror in front of her. As my nut reached its peak, I tried to pace myself with her. I wanted us to cum together. As soon as her movements, breathing and moans changed, I figured she was releasing so I finally allowed myself to release too.

As she regained her composure and was about to step into the shower she turned and replied, "Goodnight Kyle. You can keep those panties now that you've cum in them."

« Chapter 7 I Asked, She Said... »

"Lyle"

TODAY WAS THE DAY that I was going to ask for Julissa's hand in marriage. We had been going strong for over a year and I was beyond ready to tie her ass down before she got away. Everything about her screamed wifey material unlike my brother's girlfriend. That skinny heifer couldn't cook or clean.

She probably would pawn any children they had off on nannies. Speaking of my brother, I had to check his ass the other day. I had just returned from asking Julissa's dad and Aunt Kandi for her hand in marriage. They both were all for it and thought that I was the perfect man for her.

I asked my brother to take a ride with me to the jeweler. Once we got there he instantly tensed up and looked as if he were ready to go. I finally told him why we were there. I told him that I had just gotten back from asking Julissa's people for her hand in marriage and that I needed him to help me find the perfect ring for her.

I had already gotten her ring size from her aunt. He looked genuinely surprised and ask me why I'd want to do something so stupid. He then went on to say that I didn't really know her well enough and that I should explore other options.

"Other options?" I asked.

"Why in the hell would I explore other options when I've already found the most amazing woman ever created? How can I even remotely do better than Julissa? My girl is as good as it fucking gets. I'm marrying her so either you can be my big brother and help me or you can get the hell on!" I snapped.

He glared at me for a few moments before mumbling, "I guess if you're absolutely sure, I think her big-headed ass would really like that one over there."

Still mad, I took a moment to inspect the ring he'd suggested. It definitely stood out from the rest much like Julissa did.

"Yes, I think you're right. My girl would absolutely love that one. Hey Rico, let me get that one right there. I need it in a five and a half."

"You got it." Rico's deep voice boomed.

∞

"No peeking Julissa. I'm watching you woman!" I told a curious Julissa as I walked her through the dark building with a blindfold on.

"I'm not peeking. Besides I couldn't even if I tried with this hot ass blindfold on. Are we there yet???!!!"

"Almost baby. Almost." I replied.

Once reaching our destination, I sat her down, lit some candles and got down on one knee. I then told her to ditch the blindfold which she did without hesitation.

Her eyes were as big as saucers as she took in the scene surrounding her. The violinist then began to play the songs I'd requested. Tears sprang to her chinky eyes.

"Julissa, from the moment that I laid eyes on you, life as I knew it was over. You have come around and forever changed the course of my life. I could spend all day long telling you how beautiful and absolutely perfect you are for me. You are one in a million and I want to be the man who occupies your heart for the rest of your life. I want you to be the one to carry my babies.

I know we haven't known each other for years, however, I knew within days that I would eventually be down on one knee proposing to you just like this. Would you please do me the honor of making me your husband? I love you and will always honor you until our dying days baby." I vowed straight from the heart.

Julissa had tears streaming down her brown face. Her bottom lip was quivering, and snot was threatening to touch her top one. None of that even mattered to me because she was still the most beautiful woman in the world to me. Snotty and all.

"Well...say something crybaby." I joked, but was serious as hell.

"Yes, of course! Of course, I'll marry you baby! I love you so much!" She squealed.

With that she jumped up wrapping her arms around me. She plastered my face in her sweet kisses and I'd never been happier. Finally, remembering that Amy and Kyle were also present, I told Julissa she better chill out before I bent that ass over and consummated our upcoming marriage early.

I called my brother and his girlfriend over asking if they had recorded everything. Amy told me that Kyle insisted on recording the special occasion.

Kyle replied, "Of course, I got everything right here bro! That shit was really beautiful. I'm happy for you two. Now I'll finally get another nappy headed niece or nephew!" My eyes widened as we both realized what he'd just said.

He quickly cleaned it up by saying, "I meant a niece or nephew. I must be tired as hell. Too much excitement for one day."

Luckily, it didn't appear that neither Amy nor Julissa had caught on to his 'accidental' revelation. They were both too enamored by the ring me and K picked out.

"Hey K, send me that video so that I can let the world know that I am officially off the market and so is she."

"Aight cool." He said looking through his pictures and videos.

"Fuck!" Kyle quipped.

"What's up?" I inquired.

"Man bro, you aren't going to believe this shit, but I don't think I pressed the record button. Awww man, I am so sorry! Fuck!" He cussed.

"Damn K." I said disappointed.

"Hey, it's okay bro. Trust me, there isn't a single detail of this evening that I'll soon forget. It's just a video. Don't sweat it. Thanks for just being here today. I couldn't have made it through without you man. You're the best brother a nigga could ever ask for." I assured my brother while bringing him in for a hug.

I couldn't believe that I was engaged to Julissa. I vowed to spend my life making her smile the way she was that evening.

« Chapter 8 Screw Tradition »

"Amethyst"

I HAD GROWN TIRED OF Kyle jumping down my throat about needing to find a job or enrolling into school. He was seriously becoming a thorn in my ass. For the life of me, I couldn't understand why he wanted his future wife to work one of those mediocre jobs.

Additionally, why did I need to go to school when I have no intentions on using the degree. To add insult to injury, he had the audacity to throw Julissa's successful military career in my face.

When he told me that I needed to 'be more like my friend,' I felt as if he had literally punched me in the gut. My struggles and Julissa's struggles were completely different. Hell, I had tried to join the military with her years ago, but the government didn't want me. Hell, they had turned me away and they hadn't even seen my psych history.

I'd kept that tidbit to myself. I couldn't force them to take me. To pacify Kyle's nagging ass, I enrolled into an online business degree program. I figured he and I would eventually own numerous businesses together and I wanted to be a knowledgeable resource for him to come to.

This seemed to make him somewhat happy. He didn't understand why I had chosen an online program when I could've found a local program that was cheaper. I wasn't trying to be tied down to nobody's classroom.

I now had two weddings to plan. I couldn't believe that my bestie was tying the knot with Lyle. I was so happy for her although I felt a tinge of jealousy too. I wished that Kyle would man the hell up and finally wife me up.

We were going on two years strong and I had held him down the entire time. I had even cut off several of my side pieces to focus more on us. I was just down to one other man. Fuck I tried to cut him off as well, but I just couldn't afford to. Kyle wasn't lining my pockets up the way I needed him to, so until then, Denzel wasn't going anywhere.

I had been throwing Kyle hints that I was ready to get married left and right. Even Stevie Wonder could see that I was ready. I knew that after we were married, his generosity would peak. I figured he lived by the saying, never treat a girlfriend like a wife. I understood and could respect that.

Times were constantly changing, and old traditions were falling by the wayside. I had observed a growing trend on social media and had devised a plan to get my man to marry me once and for all. At first, I thought about trapping his ass with a baby. I soon learned that would prove to be nearly impossible. He was meticulous when it came to wearing condoms and he only used the condoms that he'd brought into the bedroom.

I called myself trying to be sexy one time and put a tampered condom on him with my mouth. While he had allowed me to blow him with that condom on, he removed it and applied his own before he dug into my guts.

Now, my plan was much more practical than baby trapping. In order to advance our stagnant relationship on to the next level, I was going to propose to *him*. He just had to say yes. If he didn't, at least then I'd know where we stood.

I had put in twice the time with Kyle than Julissa did with Lyle, yet she already had a huge engagement ring on her finger. I could barely stand to look at that huge rock. A rock that my man said that he'd picked out. If he had picked out a ring for her of that magnitude, I couldn't imagine how my ring would look. My baby certainly had great taste.

For starters, I had purchased us both mediocre rings with the money Denzel had blessed me with. Once he accepted my proposal, he could then purchase a ring more suitable for his queen. A huge smile swept over my face as I envisioned my boo being so happy that I'd taken the initiative to propose to him. I'm sure some men liked being chased too sometimes. Who said that a woman couldn't propose to her man?

Standing in front of my full-length mirror, I couldn't help but admire how gorgeous I looked in my wedding gown. The seamstress had outdone herself on my dress. It looked just like the one from that magazine clipping.

The train trailed behind me as I spun around in circles. My already perky breasts were lifted even higher than usual thanks to my new push up bra. How could he deny someone who looked this beautiful?

Kyle and Lyle's birthdays were next week, and Julissa and I were secretly planning a getaway for the both of them. We had rented a large two-bedroom suite in Vegas so that all of us could be close. I was so excited.

I had never been to Vegas before so I couldn't wait to see what the hype was about. I was going to propose to him there in front of Lyle and Julissa. It was only right since we were able to witness the two of them getting engaged.

Slipping out of my gown, I carefully hung my dress back up in my closet. Just as I shut my closet door, light tapping was heard at my front door. Straightening out my garter belt and hair, I went to open the front door. I smiled seductively as I allowed Denzel to brush past me. Mama had to pull out all of her tricks tonight; there was a Vegas trip that needed to be funded.

« Chapter 9 Second Chances »

"Julissa"

"DADDY! I'M HERE!" I YELLED.

I always looked forward to spending time with my dad. He had invited me over for dinner. He claimed to have something he wanted to tell me. I tried to get him to tell me over the phone, but his stubborn tail wouldn't tell me.

I spent the entire day trying to figure out what it could possibly be, but I came up with absolutely nothing. I prayed that it wasn't bad news. I just couldn't handle any bad news.

I couldn't focus at work and I had the bubble guts in anticipation of what he was going to tell me. Why the hell did people do that? Why did they leave you in suspense by telling you that they needed to tell you something, but instead of just coming out with it, they left you in limbo?

After I left work, I headed straight over to my daddy's house. I didn't bother showering or putting on my civilian clothes. Using my key to get in, I froze as I entered the family room.

Now I know that it had been many years since I had seen her, but some faces we unfortunately never forget. She still looked exactly as I remembered...even more beautiful if that was even possible. She had matured well.

Her long hair was swooped up into a neat bun. A small patch of grey hair lay strikingly on top of her head. It was somehow comforting to see how I would look in the future. There sat my egg donor smiling at me like she hadn't been missing in action for the majority of my life.

Where the hell had she been all these years? Better yet, why the hell was she here now? She was no longer needed nor was she wanted at this point. I was grown as hell. My daddy, aunts and grandparents had done a fantastic job in raising me without her.

As she continued to smile at me, I glared at her coolly. I had arrived starving and ready to chow down on an entire cow by myself, however, I had lost my appetite and was ready to go. I had no interest in faking the funk and breaking bread with that woman.

"Hi JuJu. How have you been baby girl? You are so beautiful...I just can't take my eyes off of you!" Olivia gushed.

"Hi Olivia and thanks." I said dryly.

She appeared taken aback by my cool demeanor. What the fuck was she expecting? If she was expecting me to jump up and down and leap into her arms, then she had another thing coming. As far as I was concerned, she was no different than any other stranger on the street.

"Wow JuJu, that wasn't exactly the greeting I was hoping for. I haven't seen you in forever baby. Can I hug you?" She asked.

Trying to be polite for my dad's sake, I reluctantly nodded my head. I could feel him watching our awkward exchange from the corner of my eye. She cautiously walked over to me and wrapped her small arms around my rigor mortis stiff body.

The broad had another thing coming if she thought she was about to guilt trip her way back into my life. I greeted her in the manner in which she deserved to be greeted. Plus, we hadn't seen one another in years because of *her* actions.

I allowed her to hug me until her little heart was content. When she released me, she just stared at me taking in my features. I flinched when she tucked one of my unruly strands of hair behind my ear. I had had enough of her foolishness and begun to slowly back away from her.

"I'm sorry...I was young and stupid. I'm sorry that I wasn't much of a mother to you JuJu. I'm sorry for not being there for the two of you. I've missed out on everything. I don't even know my own child." She cried as tears rushed down her face.

I awkwardly stood there looking between her and my dad. I wasn't sure what to say. Luckily, he stepped in. He walked up to Olivia and lovingly caressed her tear stained face.

My mouth was agape by the way he handled her. He was consoling her as if she weren't the enemy who had abandoned the both of us years ago. Why wasn't he tossing her out on her ass? Legal wife or not, she didn't deserve his sympathy or his love.

When my dad had tried to give her his heart, she in turn gave him her ass to kiss. I don't know what it was about my mother that made my dad's commonsense go out the window. I had never seen him so vulnerable and in love with any of the other women he had ever brought home in the past. My mother was certainly his weak spot for sure and I just did not understand why.

What was so special about Olivia?

Rolling my eyes, I decided to interrupt their little sentimental moment.

"Uhhhh dad, I think I better get going. I forgot that I had promised Amy that I'd help her with a few things." I awkwardly lied.

My dad knew better and replied, "Julissa, you will do no such thing. You see Amy nearly every day. You haven't seen your mama in years. She went through a lot to prepare your supper tonight, so go wash your hands and get ready to eat." He ordered as if I were a child.

Being the obedient daughter that I was, I went and did as

he told me to do. My dad was one of those parents that didn't care how old you got you were still to remain respectful and do as he asked you to do. Over supper I realized that Olivia was a great cook, but I wasn't going to tell her that.

I remained silent for the majority of the time that we spent together wishing that I was anywhere but there. The both of them explained that they had reconnected two years prior, however, they were reluctant to share the news with me. My dad wanted to make sure that Olivia was there to stay this time. Plus, they were *afraid* of how I would take everything.

While Olivia was probably the last woman I wanted my dad to be with, I knew it was not my place to tell him that I didn't want him to be with her. All I could do was pray that she made him happy and that this time around she proved her worthiness to him. Looking at him and how his smile reached his eyes, I couldn't help but to be happy for him. For that same reason I vowed that I would make an honest effort to get along with her.

Of course, when the time came, I would have to make it perfectly clear that I was not looking for a mother. We were way beyond that point. Perhaps we could learn to be friends in time. I didn't hate the woman who had birthed me, but I'd be lying if I said that there wasn't some resentment there.

Olivia had told me that she had been clean for four years and wanted to reconnect for some time now, but she was too ashamed and afraid of rejection to face us. She was now heavily into the church and God told her to try to make amends with both my father and me.

She stated that when she reached out to my dad, she never in a million years thought that he would be as forgiving as he had been. Her intentions were not to fall in love with him again or to make him fall in love with her all over again.

She knew that she had screwed him over in the worst ways possible. Olivia said that my dad had wanted them to fill me in on their relationship a while ago, but she had been too afraid to face me, so they continued to keep their relationship a secret.

I opened up a little with her. I discussed my career in the military, my deployment, and my love for being a pilot. I also shared with her my friendship with Amy and my engagement to Lyle. She was so extra when I flashed her my engagement ring. You would've actually thought that my ring had blinded her crazy ass by the way that she was carrying on.

I was genuinely surprised because I would've never suspected that the two of them had been carrying on for as long as they had behind my back. Who knew that my dad could be so sneaky? Prior to me leaving, I looked at them both and wished them the best in their rekindled relationship. That's all any of us could hope for, right? I also warned her that she better not hurt my daddy again.

« Chapter 10 Bros Over Hoes »

"Kyle"

TO BE ABLE TO SAY that I made it to see my twenty-third birthday was a blessing within itself. Lyle and I had lost our older brother Chance when he was sixteen and the two of us were still pissing the bed. We looked up to him and tried our damndest to emulate his swag.

He suffered from epilepsy; however, we didn't realize that he had epilepsy until it was far too late. He and his girlfriend were driving from their prom when he had begun seizing.

He ended up rear ending another car which caused his car to roll over four times. Somewhere along the way his unrestrained body was thrown out of the car. Luckily, he died instantly. The medical examiner believed that the strobe lights in the prom most likely led to the seizure. I took great comfort in the fact that Chance didn't suffer at all.

His girlfriend Danae' survived the accident and was able to tell everyone about the seizure that my brother had experienced. Danae' was left paralyzed by her injuries and unfortunately, she died two years after the accident from a blood clot that had traveled to her lungs. She was just eighteen.

Chance's and Danae's deaths scared and haunted our family for a very long time. I was a stickler about wearing seat belts and my passengers could either buckle up or get the hell out and walk.

Had Chance had his seat belt on, he very well could be alive today. I always sent God a quick prayer before driving off. I didn't know if I had epilepsy or not, but I prayed that if I did, it wouldn't manifest itself while I was driving.

On the plane ride to Vegas I had a window seat. I was able to look out above the clouds and reflect on many things. Being nearly a quarter of a century, I felt less invincible than I did the day before. Life was fleeting and it was short. I realized that maybe I was being a little too hard on Amethyst.

She truly was trying. Honestly, after she introduced me to Lissa, our relationship hadn't been the same. She didn't stand a fair chance. All I did was compare the two of them. I sought out her flaws and highlighted her shortcomings.

My brother was engaged to a woman who we both wanted, but it was time that I realized he'd won this time. I was always better than Lyle at virtually everything. It appeared that he had finally won this battle. I loved him and didn't want to lose the bond that we'd always shared...not over a female. Wasn't it bros over hoes? At least that's the way it should've been.

Finding out that the ladies had planned a weekend getaway for our birthdays had both me and my brother floored. I loved visiting Vegas, but deep down I didn't think that it was a good idea. I was trying to keep a healthy distance away from Lissa, but now I'd be occupying the same room. I was being tested to my limit.

It took everything in me to refrain from stealing glances at her at the airport as well as on the plane. I just couldn't get the images of her in the bathroom that evening out of my head.

That night had profoundly changed my love for Lissa to a full-blown obsession. She was the first person I thought about when I woke up in the morning and the last person I thought about as I fucked Amy into oblivion at night before I went to sleep.

My feelings for her were clearly unhealthy, but they had been harmless with me staying away from her. This was the first time I had seen her for longer than five to ten minutes in passing.

The first thing that I wanted to do when our plane touched down was take a quick nap. Plane rides always wore me out. The girls had gone all out on us. The suite they'd reserved was dope. It even had a private pool and waterfall. Shit, I was content with not even leaving the room at all. I could survive on room service for a few days.

Somehow, I knew Amy would never go for that. She had never been to Vegas before and wanted to do something every second that we were there. While I took a nap, her, Lyle and Lissa decided to explore the city. When I woke up, it was dark out. I couldn't believe that I had been asleep for so long. Even more shocking was that Amy had allowed me to sleep for so long.

My stomach growled loudly, and I realized that I hadn't eaten since we'd left Massachusetts. I got up and walked out of the room prepared to order me some room service. As I walked towards the kitchen area, I noticed the three of them sitting at the table whispering.

There were candles and roses all over the place and I thought it looked pretty cool. Next, I realized that all three of them were dressed like a million bucks. Looking down at myself, I was slightly embarrassed because I was still clad in my now winkled travel clothes.

I couldn't help but notice how breathtaking Lissa looked. Lyle was one lucky bastard.

Amy finally brought me out of my thoughts when she said, "Hey handsome. Come and sit beside me. We had some steaks, crab legs and lobsters delivered. I was just about to wake you up since it just came."

I gave her a warm smile and walked over to her. I leaned over her and kissed her on her succulent lips before I sat down next to her. I noticed a scowl etched into Lissa's face as she shifted in her chair. Well, look at that, I thought.

She was actually jealous. We ate and they filled me in on what they had done throughout the day. I hated that I had slept through it all, but I needed the rest.

There was always tomorrow. I had a few places that I wanted to see and several restaurants that I wanted to try out. After I stuffed my face, I thanked the ladies for their thoughtfulness. Itis was rearing its ugly head and I was ready to return back to that comfortable ass bed. Just as I let out the biggest, ugliest yawn, I noticed that Amy had stood up directly in front of me.

She didn't say anything and neither did my brother or Lissa. I was confused as fuck and just as I was about to question her, she dropped down to one knee.

I was still confused as fuck. What the hell was she doing? Had her retarded ass gotten a hold of some bad Vegas dope?

"Kyle baby, I know this isn't how it is usually done, but I've never been the average woman. I love you to the moon and back. You complete me baby. Will you marry me?" Amy asked showcasing her gleaming white teeth.

My mouth fell open. Instead of answering her, I glanced at Lyle and Lissa and they looked just as baffled as I did. I couldn't believe that that heifer had the audacity to propose to me in front of an audience.

I had been seeing her not so subtle hints all over the place, yet I chose to ignore them. I didn't feel that she was ready or that she was necessarily the one for that matter. There was only one person that I pictured myself marrying, but she was no longer on the market.

Glancing at Amy, everything in me was screaming, "Hell No! Don't Do It!"

But looking into her pretty face full of hope, I knew it had taken a lot of guts to do what she had just done. I just didn't have the heart to embarrass her in front of her best friend and my brother. I figured I'd just go with the flow for now and we'd talk in length about this once we returned home.

Lifting her chin up so that she was staring me in the eyes I replied, "Yes Amy. I'll marry you."

The rest of the evening was a blur because I immediately started chugging down shots.

« Chapter 11 Paint Me Red »

"Lyle"

IT WAS ME AND JULISSA'S WEDDING day and I couldn't have been happier. I was starting to grow frustrated and skeptical because she had pushed our wedding date back three times. At first, she decided to have a fall wedding.

Then she needed to ensure that people were able to get off work to attend our ceremony. The last excuse topped them all. She said that she'd had a dream warning her that we shouldn't get married on that particular day.

Although she had assured me that she wanted to marry me, I wasn't so sure. It was mid-October and we were set to be married at her family home. She was rebuilding a relationship with her mom and although she'd never admit it, I knew she was happy that she was involved in our wedding. I was happy for her. Everyone of course loved Aunt Kandi. I don't know why, but she looked so familiar. She was always so extra, but I loved her authenticity. You knew exactly where you stood when it came to her.

My brother, father and soon to be father-in-law were in the guest bedroom with me trying to calm my nerves and help me get my tie on just right. Was I truly ready to be someone's husband? Hell, I felt like the worst father in the world.

I couldn't even invite my own son to my wedding out of fear of my soon to be wife finding out. My son absolutely adored me and I knew he'd blow my cover. Not having him present definitely fucked with my psyche. I was dead wrong and I knew it, but what was I supposed to do?

My brother had already told me about how I wasn't shit for not including Jackson in my wedding so there was nothing anyone else could say to me that would make me feel worse than I already did.

When the time finally came to take Julissa's hand in marriage, me and her dad cried like babies. She looked like an angel on Earth in her ivory gown. The crystal covered dress was classically sexy. Its neckline plunged down to her navel.

Her tiny waist appeared even smaller since the hip area of her dress flared exaggeratedly. How the fuck did I get so damn lucky? After we exchanged our lengthy vows, we exchanged rings and were pronounced husband and wife. I felt fireworks going off as I was finally permitted to kiss the lovely bride.

Since Julissa had used all of her vacation time already, she didn't have any banked for our honeymoon. At first, I was furious that she hadn't planned better, but I got over it. Instead we had to settle for a night of passion in the new home I'd just purchased for us. I couldn't wait to ravish her body.

I have never waited so long to be with someone sexually. A couple of days to a week maybe...but never over a year! That alone further solidified the love that I had for that woman. I loved her to the degree that I did and I hadn't even hit the skins yet. This shit was definitely real.

After our reception, I swooped my bride up and sped off to the home that I was saving as a surprise for her. She absolutely loved it as I knew that she would. It was over eight thousand square feet and came equipped with all of the amenities that we could ever want or need. I couldn't wait to physically connect with her. I had never stepped out on her during our relationship, so I was beyond sexually frustrated.

I took my shower first and quickly dashed off into the bed. I impatiently waited for her to take care of her hygiene. Why did women take so damn long to get ready for bed?! After what felt like forever, Julissa came out of the bathroom with a somber look on her face. She was looking like a whole snack in the red teddy and black red bottoms I had gotten for her.

"Baby, I don't know how to tell you this, but I just started my period. I guess we will have to put our love making on hold for a week." My wife stated sadly.

"I can't believe that I didn't pay attention to my period! It was the furthest thing on my mind with all the other planning and everything going on. I'm so sorry honey." My wife continued.

"Sweetheart, you are my wife now and a little blood isn't going to kill me or you. Grab a couple of towels out of the bathroom and we will improvise." I belted out before I even realized what it was that I was proposing.

"Ewwww, no! Lyle, you are so nasty!"

"I'm so serious baby. I've waited entirely too long for this moment. I need to feel you tonight, Julissa."

After looking in my direction for a few moments as if she were in deep thought, my wife finally whispered, "Okay love. I got you."

Man, did she *have* me! Let's just say that my wife painted me red as hell that night and it was definitely worth it.

« Chapter 12 Reminiscing »

"Julissa"

IT WAS STILL HARD TO believe that I was now a married woman. To be honest, I had been afflicted by cold feet several times. I loved Lyle, I loved him dearly, but I would be lying if I said that I didn't have my doubts. He was a good man, but I sometimes wondered if we were meant to be together forever.

For starters, I had been having inappropriate thoughts and feelings for my brother-in-law. I wasn't sure why, but after my Aunt Kandi pointed out that Kyle was feeling me, it made me realize that I was in fact feeling him too. Everything about him made my cookie crumble. As scandalous as it all was, I just couldn't stop lusting after that forbidden piece of chocolate.

The night that I'd put on a show for him in my bathroom made me question my entire relationship with Lyle. I felt like such a hoe for my conflicted feelings for Kyle. At first, I didn't know that Kyle was watching me from the doorway.

I honestly thought that he had gone on his merry way. Then I somehow felt his presence and could hear his labored breathing. I was initially alarmed and questioned whether or not to put him on the spot, but for some reason I opted not to. I guess it turns out that I am into exhibitionism.

It turned me on to know that I was turning him on with my show. I envisioned that my hands were his as I paced my breathing to match his. I could tell when he was close to climaxing, so I increased the pressure and pace in which I was rubbing my clit.

I was soon standing on shaky legs as an electrifying orgasm ripped through my body. I could hear him releasing as well from behind me. I stole a quick discreet glance at him in the mirror while he was distracted and noted that he was cumming into the crotch of my panties.

That caused my clit to jump with excitement. I seductively walked over to the shower in my birthday suit.

Licking my lips, I replied, "Goodnight Kyle. You can keep those panties now that you've cum in them."

He never responded, but once I got out of the shower, he was long gone as were my panties. Instead my Aunt Kandi was sitting her drunk ass on my bed with a look of disappointment on her face. I felt so guilty that I walked over to my dresser with my head down like a child. I couldn't make eye contact with her because I knew that my ass was dead wrong. There was nothing that my Aunt Kandi could tell me to make me feel any worse than I already did in that moment.

"Juju, what did I just tell you out there? Stay away from that man, girl!" My aunt yelled.

She rarely yelled at me, so I knew that she was pissed with me. I hated disappointing my aunt because she was like a mother to me. More of a mother than my real mother had ever been.

"Auntie, I don't know what you're talking about. I didn't do anything. I just got out of the shower." I stated hoping she'd drop it, but I should've known better.

"Heifer, I have known you your entire life. I changed your shitty pampers. You cannot get a damn thing past me. With that being said, I have raised you not to be a liar. I do believe that nothing physical happened...yet.

However, you are walking a fine line between nothing and something. I saw him leaving your room...a room that he has absolutely no business being in. This shit needs to stop before it begins. Don't ever play on my intelligence again little girl!"

With that she stormed off and I heard the door slam to the guest bedroom that she was occupying for the night.

I knew that she was 100% right. I felt like a small child that had been caught with my hand in the cookie jar. She gave me a lot to think about and I knew without a shadow of a doubt that I needed to stay the hell away from Kyle Carlton. My attraction to him was undeniable. He was off limits and us together was a recipe for disaster.

I laid the towel that I had wrapped around my hot ass on the carpet. I then slid underneath my comforter in the nude. I reached over to my nightstand and opened up my second drawer.

I then retrieved my handy vibrating bullet. Hearing its low hum was like music to my ears. For the next hour I committed to wearing my ass out. I knew that Kyle was off limits physically, but there was no harm in fantasizing, right?

« Chapter 13 Girl Like Me »

"Julissa"

I'D SAY THAT MARRIED life was a little overrated, but overall good. Lyle was a great husband, at least in the beginning. Our sex life, however, typically bore me to sleep. There was no spontaneity...no spark...no ummph! It was the same old sad song and dance each night. Yes, each fucking night. Typically, most couples were allotted a five-day reprieve during Aunt Flow, but not my husband.

His sexual appetite was insatiable and as badly as I hated it on somedays, I never denied him. Not once. How could a man as endowed as my husband be such a horrible lover? He had all of that meat, yet he didn't have a clue what to do with it. Nonetheless, I was a firm believer that it was my wifely duty to ensure that he was satisfied. I knew that what one woman didn't do, another one would.

Lyle was handsome, educated, successful, and I knew that there were many women who would kill to be in my shoes. The house that my husband had purchased for us looked like something straight out of a magazine. We both stayed fairly busy throughout the day between our workdays and workouts. I loved working out with my husband. He pushed me to push myself. He was a great coach.

Everything was faring well with the exception of our mediocre love life. I wished we could incorporate a little foreplay into our routine. We literally only sexed in the missionary position and neither of us had orally pleased the other.

I was open to it, but he had previously told me that it really wasn't his thing to give or receive. I just left it at that. Xavier hadn't been into oral sex either. I couldn't miss what I'd never had so I simply just kept it moving.

My husband was anxious to start a family right away, but I was not on the same page. I couldn't imagine getting deployed again and leaving behind a child. I do not know how soldiers with children are able to cope when that occurs. I'm pretty sure I'd go AWOL. I wanted us to enjoy ourselves for at least five or so years before we brought children into the equation.

I had things that I wanted to accomplish first. I was still in my early twenties and as far as I was concerned, we had lots of time. I didn't understand what the big rush was. I sometimes wondered if that was what drove his high sex drive. I felt terrible because I had been dishonest with him about discontinuing the use of my birth control pills.

I still took them and I took them faithfully. When I was ready for us to start a family, then and only then would I ditch my birth control. After all, it was my body and I should have the final say. I only lied because he was so relentless. That was the basis of all of our arguments. He wanted a family and I truly wanted to give him one because he deserved it. But all in due time. My top priority at the moment was being a great wife and a great soldier.

My mom and I were growing closer and I thanked God for that. She was something that I didn't even know that I wanted until I had her. I can say that she was making an honest effort to make up for not being there for both me and my dad.

I had never seen him happier. He had a certain glow about him that I only seen when he was with her. Although I was against her reentering our lives in the beginning, now I was so happy that she did.

Having her in my wedding was everything. I still went to my Aunt Kandi when I needed motherly advice, but me and Olivia were getting there. She really loved Lyle for me. He adored her, too. You would've thought that he was her natural born son.

She was ready for a grandchild so both her and Lyle ganged up on me all the time. My dad naturally sided with me. He believed that I should live and see the world before I committed to having children.

He and I both knew that children changed everything. Neither Olivia nor Lyle had raised children, so they didn't understand the sacrifices required to raise children. No shade intended. I wanted to spend more time getting acquainted with my hubby.

All in all, we were blessed. So, imagine all of our surprise when Olivia called a family meeting and announced that she was in stage four renal failure. She stated that she had been battling kidney issues for years, but she had been able to keep the symptoms at bay for the most part. She was always very health conscious and particular about the foods that she put into her body, but I didn't think that it was because her kidneys were shutting down.

Of course, my dad already knew everything, but I never knew that she was sick at all. She always looked so healthy and beautiful. Now the doctors were talking about it was time for her to explore dialysis, at least until she was able to find a kidney donor. She had been added to the transplant list in the meantime.

I prayed that she found a match. The thought of losing her now that I was just getting her back drove me crazy. Of course, after much thought I told her that I was willing to donate one of my kidneys, however, she objected. She wouldn't even allow me to be tested to see if I was even compatible.

She told me that donating organs could be a disqualifier for those in the military. She refused to allow me to potentially jeopardize my career for her. She didn't feel worthy of such a gift. Although I didn't agree, my hands were tied.

Since getting married, I hadn't seen as much of Amethyst as I typically did. I still cannot believe that my girl actually proposed to Kyle. She was a hot mess! But I commended her for going after what she wanted. She was busy with planning her own wedding and completing her business degree. I couldn't be happier for her.

It was Saturday evening and Lyle was away with his brother on a business trip. I was bored out of my mind and missing having girl's night with my bestie. I picked up some wine and Chinese food for us to pig out on. I even wore one of the form fitting onesies that we both liked to relax in while we binged watched our favorite shows.

She and Kyle still hadn't moved in together and I wasn't sure why. She was always over at his house anyway. When I pulled into her driveway, I was surprised to see an all-black Bugatti Veyron. My mouth was wide open as I took in the beauty of that expensive ass car. Even if I had the money, I would never purchase such an expensive ass car, but it sure was nice to admire it from afar.

I hadn't called Amy earlier as I typically did because I didn't want to give her the opportunity to bail out on our girl's night. The logical side of me told me to turn around and go back home. However, the nosy side of me allowed curiosity to win over. I found myself balancing our food and wine in one hand while ringing her bell and knocking with the other.

After a couple of minutes with no response I finally began to call her. Growing worried after my third call went unanswered; I used my key to her place and let myself in. As I entered her house, it was extremely noisy. Music seemed to be coming from all directions as I called out to her.

Walking through her home, I sat our food on her dining room table. I then continued searching for my friend. Once I had cleared the entire house except her bedroom, I held my breath as I forcefully pushed her bedroom door open.

I gasped when I saw my best friend thrusting in and out of some high yellow obese man. I wanted to scream. I wanted to run. I wanted to throw up, yet my feet were cemented in place.

What type of freaky shit was *that* bitch on? Luckily, the music was so loud that neither of them had even seen or heard me. She was a bold bitch. If I had a key, I knew Kyle did as well. What if he had decided to come home early and caught them instead of me.

I'd then be planning my friend's funeral, instead of her wedding. As much as I loved Amy, seeing her playing Kyle that way enraged me. Don't ask, but for some odd reason I found myself snapping a couple of pictures of the two of them in action. He certainly deserved better than that bullshit. Hell, he deserved a girl like me.

« Chapter 14 E For Effort »

"Amethyst"

"OH GOD NO!!!" I shouted as my final statistics score flashed across the screen. I couldn't believe that I had failed my final!

"Damn, Kyle is going to kill me. Fuck! I should have studied." I scolded myself.

I had paid a website a lot of money to help me with my exams. They assured me that they would give me the answers to all of my tests. There were seventy-five questions, yet the website only provided me with eight of the answers.

My goofy ass was scrambling around at the last minute

trying to complete the exam with a two-hour time limit. I didn't even finish the damn test before the time lapsed.

After two hours, the exam shut off and a disappointing score of sixty-six percent jumped up on the screen. I needed at least an eighty-six percent in order to barely get a C in the class. My program didn't accept anything less than C's, so a D was as good as an F.

Now that I had bombed my statistics exam, I was officially failing two out of three of my classes. It was much too late to drop the courses, so I was going to have to eat those grades.

I didn't want any student loans, so Kyle agreed to cover whatever my grants did not. Had I listened to him and attended a local school, I would have been able to afford to pay for the classes that I had failed. The school that I attended was way too expensive for me to attempt to cover.

Kyle was bound to find out and I was afraid of that day coming. He had access to my courses and grades since he was the one who paid. That was the only downside to relying on others to support me. They were entitled to matters that I felt didn't concern them.

God, I could just hear him bitching to me now about my lack of ambition and comparing me to that God damn Julissa. Speaking of which, rewind a couple of weeks, I heard that bastard calling out her name in his sleep. I immediately woke his ass up with ice cold water to his face.

"Wake up K! Wake your ass up now!" I yelled into his wet

face.

"What the fuck man!!! What the hell did you do that for?!" His voice boomed angrily.

"Nigga have you lost your fucking mind?! You are disrespectful as fuck!" I screamed.

"Man, if your retarded ass doesn't get to the fucking point, I'm going to lay you the hell out for waking me up with this bullshit!"

"So, you are just going to lay there and pretend as if you didn't just call my best friend's name out in your sleep?!"

"Amethyst, you have officially lost your rabbit ass mind! If I was asleep, how in the fuck would I have heard myself calling out anybody's name? I swear to God; I'm getting sick of this shit. I don't know how much more of this I can take." He snapped.

"What the hell do you mean you don't know how much more you can take?! What about me? I have been spending the past couple of years trying to appease you and show you that I am the one for you. It took for me to propose to you in order for us to finally get engaged. Kyle, do you even love me? Please give it to me straight...no chaser please." I pleaded.

He stared at me for a few moments before sitting up completely. He removed his drenched shirt before redirecting his attention back to me.

"Look Amy, I care about you a lot. I may even love you...however, I do not think that I am in love with you. We are too different. We are in two different places in our lives. Neither better than the other...just different.

I think we need to slow things down a bit. I'm not saying that I do not want to be with you, but I know for certain that we are not ready for marriage. We aren't even close. You need to figure out yourself and what it is that you want.

You don't think that I know that you flunked out of school? Instead of coming to me like a real woman should, you tried to hide it like a child. Sometimes I feel like your father instead of your man. Baby, I'm not perfect...no one is. I would've understood if you were struggling in your classes. You could've gotten some tutoring to help you out had you been honest early on.

Your first mistake was going to school just to appease me. I want you to do better for you. So, to answer your question, yes, I love you, but no I don't want to marry you. At least not right now with the way things currently are. We both have some growing and self-reflecting to do." He had definitely given it to me straight just as I had asked.

His words devastated me to my very core. I felt as if someone was literally choking the hell out of me from his revelation. My lips quivered and as much as I willed myself not to cry, tears spilled from the brim of my eyes.

I loved my man and it wasn't until that very moment that I realized exactly how much. The fact that he had called out Julissa's name slipped to the rear of my brain as I tried to process where things had gone so terribly wrong between us.

I knew that I was wrong for not telling him about school, but I was just too ashamed to tell him outright. I couldn't stomach his disappointment in me. I felt like such a failure. I couldn't seem to do anything right. It was time for me to grow up and show my man that I was ready for marriage. If I needed to work and go to school, then those were the sacrifices that I was prepared to take.

I also needed to cut Denzel loose. I must have really loved Kyle if I was contemplating cutting my sole remaining sponsor off. I planned on shooting his big ass a text first thing in the morning. I was going to let him know that our little freaky ass arrangement was over. I was on my grown woman shit and it was about time he knew it. I was done with disrespecting my boo.

"I hear you baby and I completely understand. This much needed conversation has put a lot into perspective. I don't want to tell you that I'll do better, instead I'm going to show you better. I'm sorry for not being upfront about school.

I was so ashamed K. I not only let myself down, but I let you down too. I know you were rooting for me. I am going to reenroll, but this time I will attend the local classes. Apparently, I'm not disciplined enough for online classes.

Please don't give up on me or on us. I will show you that I am the only woman for you. I will make you proud of me. You'll see." I promised with sincerity etched into my pretty face.

Getting back into the bed, I crawled over to Kyle on my hands and knees. I flashed him my sexiest smile before using my teeth to untie his pajama bottoms. I then pulled them down in one swift motion. I was on my rag, but I knew that he could never resist a helping of my A1 head game. I teased him by planting kisses all over his manhood. I then smacked myself all over the face with it just to drive him crazy.

The joke was on me though because as I was about to

lightly lick the tip, he rammed his man meat all the way down my throat in one swift motion. Typically, I didn't bat and eyelash, but I wasn't prepared today.

My baby had caught me slipping. It took me a moment to regain control of the situation and when I did, I let his ass have it. All that was heard was the loud slurping of my moist mouth and him howling like a wounded animal.

One of the many things that I loved about my man was the fact that he wasn't afraid to get vocal during sex. He verbally expressed his satisfaction and I thought that shit was so hot. There was nothing worse than a nigga trying to be hard and keeping all that shit bottled up. If I was doing an amazing job, shit let me know. In return, I'd do the same.

"Oh, shit Lissa, that's right baby! Suck that big muthafucka dry!"

No, he didn't!!!

Oh, yes, his black ass did!!!

You better believe neither of us got any sleep that damn night!

« Chapter 15 Got The Juice »

"Lyle"

"YO BRO, WE DID IT! We fucking did it!!! We actually got back four times what we put into it! I guess I lost the bet and I have to take yo ashy ass to dinner." I pretended to scowl, but was internally doing the running man.

I never in a million years would've thought that the little house that I'd nearly passed on would've lined our pockets as nicely as it had. I guess it's true what they say, location was everything. Me and my brother had a rule to always agree on an investment together before pursuing a deal.

We never left one another out. I was pretty damn adamant about that house being a huge loss, but I took the risk because he wouldn't shut the fuck up about it.

As I said before, sometimes we won, sometimes we broke even, and sometimes we lost. That was the catch to real estate investments. Nothing was ever guaranteed. We literally gambled with every property that we purchased. We got that house for the low so if it had turned out to be a bust, it wouldn't have made or broke us, but I hated losing. I was in it to win it and luckily for the both of us, we had won.

"See I told your ugly ass that that little beat up muthafucka was a gold mine. Those rich folks love scooping up little historical houses like that. You have to have faith sometimes little bro."

I hated when he did that little brother shit. His monkey ass was only three minutes older than me, yet he truly acted like he was my older brother.

"Fool I did have faith. We bought that piece of shit together, didn't we? I can't hate on you this time; you got the juice. I am trying to set aside as much money as I can. Did I tell you that I'm trying to get Julissa pregnant? I've been tearing that ass up every fucking day, but her damn cervix has to be made of steel and spermicide.

I've been keeping that pussy swimming in nut, yet she hasn't even had a near miss. Her god damn period seems to come earlier and earlier than the month before. In a few months, it will be a year that we've been trying. We might have to start considering a fertility doctor to help us out. I can't wait to start a family with my wife. I already know our kids will be beautiful as hell." I revealed to Kyle.

Kyle's face was masked in a strange expression.

"Well, if the hair on her cat is as nappy as the hair on her head then no wonder why your swimmers aren't swimming to their destination." He joked.

"Stop playing! I'm being serious right now nigga. First of all, my wife has good hair and second of all she keeps that thang waxed fool! Baby smooth." I boasted thinking about the things I was going to do to her when I got home.

I didn't miss the look of lust the glazed over in his eyes. I'm sure I had the same lustful look. Was he really lusting over my woman?!

"Have you told her about my nephew yet? Please tell me you have Lyle." Kyle asked with a brow raised.

Shaking my head, I replied, "No I haven't. I don't even know how to approach it at this point. What will my wife think about becoming a stepmom overnight? Will she love him the way that I do? Will he love her as much as I do? Naw man, I've been thinking. I am going to tell her after she gets pregnant. That way it will make it harder for her to just leave my ass. I know she isn't about that single parent life."

It was becoming incredibly difficult to hide them from one another. During the weekends when I spent time with my son, I felt guilty because I always had to come up with excuses as to why I couldn't spend time with her.

On the rare occasions when I had to cancel seeing my son, it was always a big to do with my son's mom. I hated hearing that bitch's mouth. She truly didn't comprehend the concept that shit sometimes doesn't work out the way we planned.

I longed for the day that my son and wife were under the same roof. I knew the longer that I put off telling my wife, the worse the possible consequences were bound be. Hopefully one of my seeds found their target soon. I hated sneaking around, but I had to for the moment for a lack of other choices. I just prayed that she made the right decision because I refused to live without her. She was mine. All mine.

« Chapter 16 Call Me What You Want »

"Kyle"

I COULD'VE BODY SLAMMED my brother for rubbing Lissa in my face! I was fuming as he bragged about sexing the woman that I felt I deserved. I loved him dearly, but he was a lame. He didn't know what a woman of her caliber needed. She needed a deeper love that I wasn't sure he was capable of giving her.

I craved her constantly. Every time I rolled over in my California king bed, I was disappointed when I spotted Amy lying beside me. Lissa and I deserved each other. We were meant for one another. Julissa was tormenting me even in my sleep. Me and my girl were still beefing over that shit.

After calling Amy by Lissa's name while she was giving me dome, she went off! I was definitely slipping. I had never done any crazy shit like that before. Had a nigga afraid to fall asleep and shit.

I haven't even sampled Lissa's pussy outside of its scent and I was already feeling all the backlash behind it. Amy was now convinced that I wanted her best friend...which of course we all knew that to be true. But, she didn't need to know all of that.

I was experiencing some major resentment against both my brother and Amy. They were both standing in the way of me and Lissa's happiness. After going back and forth with Amy that night, we took each other's keys back. We were starting back at square one in our relationship. I couldn't stand constantly being accused of some shit that I didn't do. I was not about to be condemned on a daily basis when all I had done was sniff some damn drawls.

I busied myself with work and she and I met up a couple of nights out of the week to have dinner together and fuck. As I said before, her sex game was on point, but it wasn't worth all of the grief she was giving me.

I had completely cut Amy off financially. When I had tried to help her, she had taken me for granted. Now it was time for her to level up and prove that she could be self-sufficient. Beauty just wasn't enough. There were tons of beautiful women in Massachusetts.

When I went over to Amy's house to return all of the items that she had remaining over at mine, she made a point to show me her enrollment papers from the community college. She also produced a name badge from Walmart.

I was very proud of the strides she was making to get her life in order. It appeared that she was making an honest effort this time around. She was enrolled in school full-time and was working full-time as a cashier.

With her new schedule, I realized that she was less of a bugaboo. Productivity was *everything*. She was never particularly too overbearing, but now with her slightly out of the picture I was enjoying the free time. The days following me calling out Lissa's name was crazy. She was up my ass like white on rice until we agreed to our current situation.

Please don't get me wrong. I am not by any means trying to minimize how fucked up what I did truly was. But it was out of my control and the deeds were done. I couldn't go back and change the shit because if I could have, I would have. She basically needed to get over it or set me free. I was done apologizing.

Whoever our invisible cupid was sucked at their job. We were clearly set up with the wrong women. My brother always bitched about Lissa being in the Air Force and how he was against her going back to school.

Hearing that type of shit made my dick hard and my heart swell for her even more. She was exactly the type of woman I needed. Shit, Lyle could have Amy's lazy, unmotivated, money hungry ass! She would love to be home all day doing absolutely nothing, but ordering from Amazon Prime.

Unfortunately, I knew she wouldn't even keep him happy because she couldn't cook, and she kept her house messy as fuck. She wasn't a sink full of dishes type of nasty, but she just had clothes, shopping bags and random shit just scattered about. My brother was a neat freak. He would kill Amy's ass.

I wasn't as meticulous as my brother, but I was definitely no Amy when it came to tidiness. I was a firm believer that everything had its place. Our mother had taught us early on not to rely on a woman to feed us or clean for us. We were both great cooks and maintained clean houses.

How could I make Lissa see that she belonged to me and not Lyle? I know they were already married and shit, but it wasn't too late for an annulment. I needed to get her away from him before he knocked her up. He was hyper-focused on getting her pregnant in order to keep her from leaving in the event that she found out about my nephew.

Knowing what I knew, I couldn't allow the love of my life to go out like that. She deserved to know the truth and I didn't think she'd ever get the truth from Lyle. My brother was a scary nigga and always avoided conflict. I welcomed conflict to dinner quite often. There was no bitch in me.

Some lies were being told and it was time for the truth to set my brother's bitch ass free. Call me what you want, but his day of carrying his happy ass home to my woman were numbered. Her nappy headed ass belonged with me and I had no intentions on stopping until she was mine. It was definitely time for Lissa to meet little Jackson and Kamisha! Fuck Lyle and fuck Amy too!

« Chapter 17 Decisions »

"Lyle"

"I CANNOT WAIT TO finally see your beautiful face baby. I know it has only been four days, but it seems like forever. I can't stand to be away from you, but I hope that you're enjoying yourself down there. But don't have too much fun, I don't want to have to hurt anyone down there for trying to take what is mine" I threatened.

I wasn't sure if she realized whether or not I was serious, but I was dead ass serious. I would kill a muthafucka dead over my wife without any remorse. She was completing some training down in Texas for the military and I hated that shit. When she returned, I planned on sitting her down and having a heart to heart about her future plans. I prayed that her future did not include the Air Force.

We needed to square this shit away once and for all. I was constantly on edge dreading the day when my wife would be deployed again. The military had invested a lot of money into Julissa and I knew sooner or later they would pounce down on our little family ready to get their monies worth out of her. Why couldn't she see why this was upsetting to me? Our previous conversations regarding the Air Force went absolutely nowhere.

How can you convince someone to leave the military when they felt that it was their calling? She'd always give me the same song and dance about how she had come from a long line of Airmen and had always wanted to be one as well. She told me that she wasn't 100% sure, but she was quite certain that she wanted to make a career out of the military.

Quite frankly, I was sick and tired of competing with the government for my wife's affections. She was always on the go and never had a moment's rest. It was no wonder that she couldn't get pregnant, her stress levels had to be high. To top it all off, she announced that she was considering going back to school for engineering like her dad.

It was funny how the very things that had initially attracted me to her were the very things that now drove me crazy. She was ambitious to a fault. I just wanted a sexy little housewife who was as good in the kitchen as she was in the bed. Sexually my wife was everything that I could ever hope for. I was fairly conservative and while sex was pleasurable, I believed that it was primarily done for procreating.

I didn't need all of those fancy positions to get me off. A good wet twat was enough for me. I was easy to please. I wanted a big family too. Five maybe six mini-me's. At some point I wanted to gain full custody of my son, too. I didn't want him to ever feel excluded...like an outcast within our family dynamic.

Deep down I knew that Julissa was not on the same page. Hell, she wasn't even in the same book as me! We needed to discuss the best way to go about compromising so that we were both able to get what we wanted from one another. That's what marriage was all about. We were both going to have to bend a little.

She had three years left in her new contract and during that time I would try my hardest to convince her to choose me first. Between the Air Force and her talks of returning to school, it was hard for me to ignore the elephant in the room. Where would that leave us? Would she still cook, keep the house tidy, sex me every night, and make time for us?

"What time is your flight landing tomorrow?" I asked her through the phone. At the same time, my son had fallen and let out a piercing cry.

I panicked.

I didn't know whether to run and comfort my hardheaded son or to immediately hang the phone up on my wife before she began questioning the noise in the background.

It was too late as she asked, "Baby, what is that? Do you have a baby over there with you?"

"What? Why would I have a baby over here with me? Woman that's the damn tv. But hey listen, I have to take care of a few things, but I'll be at the airport to pick you up bright and early." I told her.

"Okay, be there by 8:00 am. I can't wait to see you. I love you so much. See you tomorrow babe." She responded.

"I love you too. I'll see you at 8. Bye."

"Bye baby."

I felt horrible because the entire time that I was wrapping things up with my wife, my son had been screaming his head off. I finally went into daddy mode and rushed over to console my child. I panicked when I noticed the golf ball sized goose egg on the back of his head.

"Oh my God! I'm so sorry man. Daddy is so sorry!" I consoled him with a heavy heart.

I didn't know much about first aid or anything, but I knew that I needed to apply some ice to his head and keep him awake. I sat him down in a chair and went to work. I first cleaned his face off with one of his baby wipes.

The whole time I talked to him and got him to laugh. Handing him a Popsicle, I grabbed a sandwich sized Ziplock bag and filled it with ice. I scooped my son up and brought him into my brother's living room. I turned on his favorite cartoon and sat him on my lap.

I held the ice bag in place for what seemed like forever. I texted my mom and asked her if she felt that I needed to take him to the hospital or to the urgent care and she told me no. She said that if he starts to act differently, started swallowing excessively or developed an unusually running nose then I should take him to be evaluated immediately. She also instructed me to find a black permanent marker and to outline the lump to monitor whether or not it was getting larger.

I trusted my mom's judgement; after all she had raised three boys who all thought they were invincible. As I cared for my son, I felt bad for my mother and the hell that I knew the three of us had put her through. We were always breaking bones and stressing her out with our concussions and abrasions.

She was the real MVP! As I held my son, I couldn't help but to wonder what me and Julissa's babies would look like. I wished like hell that he was Julissa's. With her soft, nurturing nature, I knew that she was going to be an amazing mother to our children one day.

Today was a close call...in fact too close. I hated myself for ignoring my injured child just to save face with my wife. I know that I could've used that moment to come clean to her, but it just never seemed like the right time.

Having to choose between my seed and my wife was a turning point and something I didn't care to have to do again. I knew that I needed to get everything out in the open before shit really got ugly. Yes, something had to give.

« Chapter 18 Closed Mouths Don't Get Fed »

"Julissa"

I THOROUGHLY ENJOYED myself down in Texas. The warm air was a nice welcome from the bone chilling weather we had in Massachusetts. Don't get me wrong, I loved my city and all, but the freezing temperatures were sometimes disrespectful.

The Texas accents had me dying with laughter. I had always gotten a huge kick out of their southern drawl and country lingo. I thought it was cute though.

The trip had also given me a much-needed break from my horny ass husband. I swear that man took Viagra or something! My pussy stayed sore because he never took the time to warm me up beforehand. He just crawled his ass in between my thighs and pushed himself inside of me. Trust me when I tell you, my husband was packing downstairs! It was no easy feat taking all that sausage every day especially with no preparation.

I know that I could have told him no, but I loved the little bit of intimacy that our love making brought about. I was going to talk to Aunt Kandi to see if I could bounce some ideas off of her about the best way to approach him about being more spontaneous in the bedroom.

I was tired of pretending to be satisfied sexually. I had only been with two men and they were both duds in the sack. This couldn't possibly be the reason why people loved sex so much. It just had to get better than this.

This couldn't be what the romance novels fixated so deeply on. I wanted my husband to make me feel the way the love songs on the radio made me feel. I dreaded having this conversation because what man wanted to hear that his sex was boring?

Making love was cool sometimes, but I wanted Lyle to fuck me as well. I wanted him to eat me out for the first time. I wanted him to bend me over and fuck me into oblivion. Was that asking for too much? I personally thought my request was reasonable and obtainable.

My Aunt Kandi was all about me giving it to Lyle straight. She told me that if I didn't feel comfortable addressing my husband verbally, then I should just take the initiative in the bedroom.

"As fine as my nephew-in-law is, he can't be that bad niece!" Aunt Kandi squealed being extra as usual.

"Auntie...it isn't bad, it's worse! I should've won several

Oscars by now for this year's best orgasm faker!" I exclaimed defeated.

"You do know that you are partially to blame for this, right?" She suggested.

"How am I to blame for this travesty?" I inquired.

"A marriage is a fifty-fifty partnership, correct?" She asked for clarity.

"Yes ma'am, it is." I confirmed.

"Well, there is nothing you should be afraid to sit down and talk to your partner about. A lot of this shit should have been discussed during the dating phase. While I'm happy that the two of you waited to have sex until after marriage, this is the problem many people who do decide to wait often face.

You don't know what you're getting until after you've gotten it. Oftentimes your partner doesn't live up to your expectations and that's okay...just don't pretend that they are. That's where your fault in this comes into play.

You should've never started this charade. How can Lyle fix some shit that he already thinks is on lock? Your orgasm faking ass has him falsely walking around feeling like the original Casanova!

Instead of giving that man pseudo-orgasms, you should have been telling him what it is that you do like. Tell him what makes you feel good. Tell him what makes your toes curl niece. You are in this marriage for the long haul and it is only fair that the *both* of you are sexually satiated.

Otherwise, you and I both know that you will eventually venture off into other territories. Trust me, you don't even want to start your marriage off on that note. You guys are still in the honeymoon phase baby girl. Teach him how to love you Juju." My Aunt coached.

I sat in silence for a while trying to process all of the wisdom my dear aunt had laid upon me. I just loved that woman so much. I still wasn't quite comfortable with having sensitive conversations like this with Olivia, but I knew that in the future we'd have our own unique bond. My Aunt Kandi never married, and I never understood why because she was such an amazing person.

"Okay Auntie, I will make a pit stop at Life's Little Pleasures after I leave here. It is worth a shot if it will save my marriage. I'll do anything to have my husband get me off for once." I sighed full of hope.

I felt a thousand percent better after speaking to my aunt. Why didn't I think of this on my own? I was always so submissive sexually with my husband, hell Xavier, too, for that matter. It was time for me to dominate and take the lead for once.

I called Amy to see if she was down for a trip to Life's Little Pleasures. She answered on the second ring. The two of us had actually been hanging out more lately. I never brought up what I had witnessed in her bedroom that fateful night either. I wasn't even sure how to form the words to ask my best friend what the hell that shit was about.

Why in the hell would she be butt fucking that fat funky ass slob when she had Kyle to knock boots with? There were just too many questions marks swirling around in my head. If I knew my girl correctly, I was certain that his yellow ass was spending some major cash on her. There was no other explanation for the fuckery that I had witnessed that night.

I knew, that she knew, that I knew though. My retarded ass had flown out of there like a bat out of hell and it wasn't until I made it all the way home that I realized that I had forgotten the food and the wine on her table. She was a smart cookie so I'm sure that she had connected the food with my incessant calls and text messages and put two and two together.

She knew that I had seen that crazy shit. It's funny how we had been hanging out more since that incident. I wondered if she was keeping closer tabs on me just to see if I would throw her under the bus to Kyle, but she was my girl and I'd never do that to her. Hell, I had no room to judge. After all, it was her man that I was lusting over.

∞

Amy told me that she would meet me at the adult sex store in thirty minutes and then we'd have lunch together. Once we reached the sex store; I had filled Amy in on the conversation that I'd had with my Aunt Kandi. Amy already knew about my sexual woes and her advice was fairly similar in nature. She had told me to just sit on Lyle's face.

Although I desperately wanted to, his potential reaction and the fear of rejection took over. I had found a couple of sexy teddies, a see-through jump suit, some hand cuffs, blind folds, massaging oils, a clit stimulator and some edible panties. Nervous jitters coursed through me as I thought about what tonight had in store for me.

Amy stated that she already owned half the damn store, so she really didn't purchase much for herself. My friend was a freak, so I knew she was speaking nothing but the truth. After I was satisfied with my items, we left in our vehicles and I followed her to South End to an amazing place called Southern Proper. They were known for their amazing southern cooking.

I rubbed my hands together in anticipation of the marvelous meal that I was about to receive. We were seated and promptly asked for our drink orders. I was so hungry that I ordered my drink and my meal at the same time. I didn't mess around when it came to my food. I ate a lot, however, I worked out a lot as well. Me and Amy both ordered their chicken and waffles brunch special.

Amy and I shot the breeze as we waited on our meals. She had told me that she and Kyle had been having some fights lately over a few different matters. For starters, apparently, she thought that he was messing around on her. Not only had he said another woman's name in his sleep, but he also called her by that same name while she was sucking him off.

To say that my bottom lip hit the floor would be an understatement. I couldn't believe that he had disrespected her to such an infinite degree. Between me and you, I was a little salty too.

I almost felt as if he was messing around on me as well. Who was this new woman? I did ask Amy if she recognized the name of the person that he had called out, and she was very short when she told me that she did.

I didn't pry any further. I couldn't imagine how she felt. I would kill Lyle's ass. My girl was going through it! She told me that she had flunked out of school and that she had tried to hide it from Kyle.

Unfortunately, he found out and had temporarily postponed their engagement. I truly did feel horrible for my friend. No wonder why she had been MIA. She had been going through it and I hated that I wasn't there for her.

I told her that he would come around in time. They were still together so that meant that he still had strong feelings for her. If he didn't care, he would've simply just walked away. After we conversed some more over our food, we both left feeling more optimistic about our futures

« Chapter 19 A Little Extra »

"Lyle"

OPENING MY FRONT DOOR, I entered my home with the weight of the world on my shoulders. I was exhausted as hell and my mind was going one-hundred miles per hour. I had just had one of the longest and most stressful days that I'd had in a really long time. Me and Kyle had recently underestimated the cost to fix up one of our properties.

There was a lot more work needed than anticipated. We would be lucky if we turned a five-thousand-dollar profit after labor and supplies. It was hardly worth the time we'd invested into it. Of course, it was one of the houses that I insisted that we took a chance on. Now I had my brother all over my ass about the shit.

I know some of you are thinking at least we turned a profit and that it was better than nothing. While five thousand dollars may have impressed us in the very beginning of our hustle, it was nothing, but pocket change to us now. Especially considering that we had to divide that by two.

But that's not even the half. We received a call from one of our tenants who had been out of town for the holidays. She came back and apparently the pipes had frozen and then burst, flooding the house. Sure, we had homeowner's insurance on all of our properties and mandated that all of our tenants maintained renter's insurance, but it was still all a pain in the ass.

I had planned on spending the next day with my wife, but now my brother and I had to get up at the ass crack of dawn to meet the insurance assessor. I hadn't seen my son since he had fallen because his stupid ass mother told me that she didn't feel that he was safe with me anymore.

I really wanted to kill her ass. I had never been away from him for this long and it was killing me. His mama had also found out that I was married I'm assuming via social media so that gave her even more ammunition to not allow me to see my son.

It was always some bullshit! I just wanted to eat, shit, take a hot shower, make love to my wife and then go to sleep. I wished that I could redo the entire day over, but with a different outcome of course. Walking through my foyer, I could instantly smell the cleanliness of my home followed by something delicious that my wife had prepared.

Looking down, I was pleasantly surprised when I saw a trail of roses. I followed the roses towards my bathroom in anticipation. Reaching the end of the trail of roses, I cracked the first smile that I'd had that entire day when I saw that Julissa had prepared a nice bubble bath for me. It looked so soothing. My baby had even taken the liberty of preparing me a glass of wine on the side of the tub.

I disrobed wondering what else she had in store for us that night. Thoughts of her quickly overshadowed my shitty day. As I sat down in the tub, I instantly felt my body loosen up. Marsha Ambrosius' Late Night & Early Mornings was playing in the background.

I was fixated on watching the flames of the candles dance when my wife seemingly glided like a cat into the bathroom. I swear she had the sexiest walk ever. She reminded me of a black panther with her seductive strides.

As I studied her attire, I instantly hardened. Julissa was wearing a fire engine red teddy. It was completely see-through in the tit area. It was also crotchless and I noticed that the back was merely a thong.

She had straightened her normally curly hair, so this made her look extra sexy. Her six-inch stilettos made her petite frame stand nice and tall. I was ready to abandon my tub and release some of my stress off into my wife. Julissa walked up behind me and began to give me her signature massage.

Her tiny hands possessed magic in them. My head fell back onto her breasts as I reveled in her love. Once she was finished giving me the best massage of my life, she took my wine glass and served it to me.

My wife then took my washcloth and carefully washed my body from head to toe. I always enjoyed the attention that she showered me with. She was so amazing. Once my bath concluded, I stood up and allowed her to dry me off and apply lotion to my skin. I then followed her to our bedroom. Our bed was covered in rose petals too.

"Lay down." She commanded.

I wasn't sure what had gotten into my wife, but so far, I liked it. I laid down as she had instructed me to. First, she applied handcuffs. I had initially objected but in the end, I decided to trust my wife. She then put a blindfold on me. I wasn't with that shit either, however I just went with it. My wife then committed to teasing me with feathers and light kisses in various places.

I felt her licking on my nipples which felt great. She licked all around my belly button too. Once she took my dick into her mouth, I lost control. Her lips were pillow soft and warm. I had received some horrible head as a teenager that scarred me for life. The girl that was sucking me off didn't know what the hell she was doing, and her braces and teeth cut the hell out of my dick.

Since then, I haven't been into head. That pain was something that I never wanted to experience again. My wife, however, changed that shit on that night. I couldn't comprehend how something could feel so amazing. She was doing an amazing job for an amateur. I was close to climaxing when she abruptly stopped.

Then she resumed, only to stop again once I grew close to cumming. I was losing my mind. Had I not been handcuffed; I would've taken the pussy already. Instead I laid there in complete darkness as my wife took advantage of my body.

At some point I felt her releasing the handcuffs and removing my blindfold. She then laid on her back with her legs spread eagle. She began rubbing on her clit which was something that I had never seen her do before.

"Baby, I know you aren't into giving oral, but do you think that you can make an exception for tonight?" She asked.

I couldn't believe that she was asking me to do that nasty ass shit! Blood, discharge and humans came out of pussies, yet she wanted me to put my mouth on it! Do you know that feeling that you get when your mouth produces extra saliva just before throwing up?

Well that's the exact reaction that I was experiencing, but I tried to maintain my composure. She had gone out of her way to make sure that I had a pleasurable time this evening, it was only fair that I returned the favor. Right?

Julissa was always so giving and rarely ever asked for anything. Although, it went against what I was in to...how could I deny someone as self-less as her? Without saying a word, I closed my eyes and lowered my face down towards her pussy.

It wasn't until my nose brushed up against her pubic bone that I realized that I had reached my destination. Peeking out of one eye, I half ass stuck my tongue out. After much contemplating, I gave her labia one swift lick and lost it.

I jumped up and told her that I just couldn't do it. I felt so horrible. So embarrassed. My brother gave me shit about it all the time. Even then, my wife tried to make me feel better.

"It's okay baby. I understand. Baby steps. I bought this new lubricant that gets cool and then warm. I'm going to put it on your dick and then I want you to bend me over and fuck me like you've never fucked me before, okay?"

I nodded and smiled at the fact that she was still going to give me some pussy. Julissa took the tube of lube and squeezed a decent amount of it into her hand. After rubbing her hands together, she then began to stroke my dick. The sensation was different. I definitely felt my dick alternate in between coolness and warmth. After my stick was coated nicely with the lube, my wife eagerly assumed the doggy style position.

As I grabbed my dick, and prepared to enter my wife from the back, I realized that something just didn't feel right. When I glanced down at my dick, I nearly had a heart attack and croaked. My dick was literally covered in lube covered bumps. My shit looked like a God damn Nestle crunch bar.

The moment that I saw my shit all lumped up, it instantly felt as if a thousand fire ants were biting and crawling on my dick. I don't know why seeing shit actually made the injury feel worse.

"What the hell Julissa?! What is in that shit?!" I asked in a panic.

Sensing my fear, she hopped off the bed and all I heard was, "Ahhhhhhhhhh! Baby, what's wrong?! What happened to you?!"

Her eyes were huge as she looked at me with concern.

"Where is that lube? I need to read the ingredients!" I yelled unintentionally.

She flinched and then ran over to the nightstand and retrieved it. She immediately handed it over for me to read.

As I scanned over the list of ingredients, I spotted two of my allergens. I was allergic to the Benzocaine as well as the Capsaisin. I should've known better than to allow her to rub some foreign shit on my body like that. I guess I was caught up in the moment and I was trying to appease my wife after letting her down.

"Baby, do you want me to take you to the emergency room?" Julissa asked.

"Hell no! I'm not walking in that muthafucka with a

lumpy dick! I'm about to take some Benadryl and a cold shower. Hopefully that will do the trick."

"I'm so sorry baby. I forgot all about your allergies."

"It's okay love. That's what I get for acting a little extra earlier."

« Chapter 20 Ultimatums »

"Amethyst"

I LOVED KYLE AND all, but he had me all the way fucked up! I just didn't understand him or this bullshit arrangement he insisted that we make. We fought and we fought about it, but in the end, I just agreed to the terms of his ultimatum. What other choice did I have?

Basically, all I heard was get a job, go to school or it's over. So here I was basically working at Walmart for peanuts. Wearing that uniform for the first time was one of the most embarrassing things I've ever had to do.

Here I was, a woman beautiful enough to be a runway model, flouncing around in that cheap ass blue vest. I prayed on a daily basis that I didn't run into anyone that I knew. I would just die where I stood if that happened. Each day that I stood on my sore feet scanning those welfare recipients' food, I grew to resent Kyle more and more. Sure, I still loved my man, but he was going to pay for putting me in that predicament.

School wasn't much better. It was boring as fuck and those classes were painfully long. I thought high school sucked, but college took the cake. Since I was one of the older students, the shit felt like high school most days.

I would just show up with my resting bitch face on and sit all the way in the back. I spent most of the time pigging out on food I'd copped from the vending machines or browsing social media sites.

So far, I was passing all of my classes. Despite hating school, I was definitely studying this time around. I needed my man to realize that I had seen the error of my ways. Then maybe he'd resume my prior privileges.

His black ass had the audacity to take my key and credit card! I mean, the card only had a two-thousand-dollar limit, but since I relieved Denzel of his financial duties, shit has been hard for me. Did I mention that my job didn't pay shit?

By working full-time, I was putting my social security check in jeopardy as well. I was working way more than someone receiving benefits was allowed. I was taking a huge risk, because I knew in the end, the payout would be so much sweeter. Being Mrs. Amethyst Carlton would give me access to boat loads of money. That social security check was a necessary sacrifice that needed to be made.

The situation between Kyle and I was getting to me so much so that I went to talk to my mother about it. Since her fat ass was the queen of making the best out of shitty circumstances, I hoped that she could give me some insight into how to get my man to see shit my way. I hadn't seen her since my dad's funeral last year and I almost immediately regretted seeing her now.

Entering her house was like walking through a scene from the show Hoarders. I was raised in filth. We were the family that dressed well and had expensive shit due to her endless schemes, yet we were rarely allowed to have company over. I can't remember not having roaches. Hell, my little brother Kylon even had a roach crawl into his ear while he slept one night.

He kept crying and telling her and the school nurse that something was crawling in his ear canal. Of course, the school nurse didn't have the proper equipment to look deep down into his ear, so she called and sent a note home with Kylon for mama to take him to the emergency room.

It took my mama's lazy ass a week to finally take him seriously and take him to the emergency room. Luckily, they were able to extract it without any damage. It was dead by the time they had removed it.

You'd think the roach in the ear situation would have been enough to make mama clean up more. We were young and did what we could, but it was her endless shopping and collecting that took over our home.

She simply told all of us to start sleeping with cotton balls in our ears. I was terrified of that shit happening to me for many years to come. Sometimes I still slept with cotton in my ears, if I was in an unfamiliar place.

When I walked into mama's house, the stench of stale cigarette smoke, feet, and fat folds infiltrated my nostrils. My face immediately scrunched up in disgust. I hated visiting that bitch.

"Ma!"

"In the living room girl! Stop all that yelling!"

I rolled my eyes as I squeezed through the tiny path leading to the living room. There was so much shit everywhere that I feared a rodent would run across my new Jimmy Choo boots.

"Hey ma, how are you?" I asked dryly.

"I'm okay. About time you came to visit your mama. It's ironic ya know? I can't get your lazy ass brothers or sister to leave, yet I can't get you to come over. You're gonna miss me when I'm gone little girl." Her dramatic ass whined.

"I'm sorry ma. I've just been going through a lot. I'm working full-time and taking classes for my business degree. Plus, my fiancé...or at least I think he is has been giving me the blues." I stated.

She looked me up and down and replied, "Well, you look good girl. Life's been kind to you it appears." She replied sadly in an envious tone ignoring my previous comment.

"Oh, if only you knew the half, ma."

I spent the next twenty minutes filling her in on my troubles and asking her what she would do if she was in my shoes.

She essentially told me that I needed to create a wedge between Kyle and Lyle. In doing so, Kyle would never have a reason to be around Julissa. While I didn't believe that my girl would do me like that...Kyle was definitely feeling some type of way about her. I wasn't taking any chances.

Just as she finished schooling me, my brother Travis walked in. It was in that moment that I decided to hit Kyle in his wallet and make him pissed off at his brother all at the same time. I was all for killing two birds with one stone.

I remember overhearing Kyle telling Lyle that he thought that a house that they had just snagged was a huge risk. He didn't think that it was a good purchase. The two of them went back and forth for a while before I heard him tell Lyle that he trusted his judgement since he had recently taken a leap of faith on him.

He told his brother that he was going to go with the flow. He also told him that if they ended up taking an L then he was going to kick his ass before hanging up on him.

A light bulb went off in my head. Travis was an out of work construction worker who would do just about anything for a buck. He didn't like Kyle anyway for firing him. My brother had inherited my father's alcohol addiction, but the boy was great at what he did. He had missed one too many shifts for Kyle's liking and he was canned. No amount of bomb ass head was able to persuade him to give my brother his job back.

I filled my brother in on the risky house deal that my man and his brother made. I wanted Travis to get into the house as it was being rehabbed and inconspicuously fuck some shit up. I wanted it to appear as if the shit had been fucked up all along, but just overlooked.

I didn't know a damn thing about houses, but I knew that my brother could cause thousands of dollars' worth of damage. This would also push the completion date back and the amount spent towards parts and labor would increase.

If that didn't piss Kyle off at his brother, I didn't know what would. I also told my brother about their tenant Mrs. Jefferson going out of town for the holidays. The temperature in Massachusetts was predicted to dip to a record breaking low.

So, I told him to make it appear as if the pipes had busted and to flood the old bitch's house. I hated to involve innocent people, but she never liked me anyway so fuck her senile ass too.

I know you all are being all judgmental and thinking I'm a fucked-up individual for doing this, but that nigga started it. He didn't have to do me the way he had. Now he was going to suffer the consequences for his actions.

« Chapter 21 No Breeders For Me »

"Kyle"

"HEY KYLE, I'M SORRY TO disturb you, but I couldn't get a hold of that husband of mine. Have you seen him?" Lissa's sexy voice spoke into my ear.

She never called me, and I was shocked that she even had my number. I felt like a weak ass teenager giddy from just the sound of her voice through the receiver.

"Oh hey, what's up Harriet Tubman? I haven't heard from you in a while. Do you still have your edges?" I teased.

"Oh, just forget it! I'm hanging up now!" She snapped.

"Whoa whoa...wait! Damn you are in a mood today. Is it

that time of the month?" The line was silent, so I feared she'd hung up on me.

"Hello?" I called out.

"Why do you play so much Kyle? Do you even know how to be serious? I'm not in the mood to play with you today. I'm looking for my husband. The water heater...furnace or something broke and this house is so cold that I can see my God damn breath!" She said emotionally.

"Well Lissa, you know me and that nigga aren't exactly seeing eye to eye at the moment so I don't know where he is these days." I partially lied.

We really weren't talking much these days, but I still loved my nephew. I always looked forward to spending time with him. It wasn't his fault that his daddy was a cowardly moron. I knew that Kamisha was tired of having to watch my nephew on the weekends and had started allowing Lyle to see Jackson again.

My brother always made it seem as if he worked on the weekends when the truth was, he was over at my house with my nephew. I knew that he probably wasn't answering because he didn't want Lissa to hear Jackson's hyperactive ass in the background.

Since I wasn't home, I knew that Lyle wouldn't be able to rush home like she needed him to because of Jackson. I was actually out getting him his favorite cereal when Lissa called.

"I'll tell you what, I'm about ten minutes away. I'll stop by and check it out." I heard her saying something, but I quickly hung up before she could object.

I tell you that I turned that ten-minute ride into a three minute one, you better believe it. I checked my breath before pressing the doorbell.

My grown ass was actually getting butterflies as I anticipated Lissa opening the door for me. When she did, my heart stopped for a moment. She had somehow managed to get even more beautiful since the last time I had seen her.

Her hair was straightened, and her new blonde highlights suited her perfectly. She was bundled up in what appeared to be ten layers of clothing, a robe and toe socks, yet her natural beauty exceeded Amy's "beaten" face any day. Staring at her from her doorway made me hate my brother even more.

I sucked it up and gave her a warm smile and a hug. I didn't want to creep her out, so I released her within a reasonable amount of time. She smelled so fresh and clean without any overwhelming perfumes.

I walked past her without an invitation and headed straight to their utility closet that housed their water heater. To be honest, their house was so cold that I was pretty sure that it was warmer outside. I assessed the water heater for less than a minute and realized that the pilot light had simply gone out. All it needed was to be relit. I wasn't going to tell her ass that though.

I relit the pilot light, but did not turn the heat on right away. I fiddled around and pretended to be busy for a while. In the meantime, she had fed me and we had a good time joking and laughing at various things.

As I went to finally turn on the heat, it was one of the saddest moments of my life. I knew my time with her was coming to an end. The heat kicked in almost instantly and she was ecstatic. I knew I needed to leave because I had been gone for far too long.

She walked me to the door and she thanked me again. I looked into her eyes and took my right hand to swipe her stray strands of hair to the side. When she didn't stop me, I slowly placed my lips on top of hers. Her velvety lips felt like heaven. My dick was trying its damndest to push its way through my jeans. Here we were making out like a couple of teenagers in her doorway for all to see.

Luckily, it was cold out so there wasn't a soul around. When I palmed her soft ass, she finally pushed me away.

"I love you." I boldly admitted.

She cleared her throat and stared down at her ugly ass toe socks.

"I said, I love you Lissa. I know you love me too. Leave that clown. Please." I pleaded throwing caution to the wind.

I know that I had no right and that I was wrong on so many levels, but I was tired of going home to an empty house every day.

Finally looking up at me she said, "Kyle you need to leave and please do not return unless my husband is here."

That comment struck a nerve and I was as hot as volcanic lava.

"Man Lissa, fuck that nigga! I know your bored as fuck with his non-fucking ass! Hit me up when you are ready for me to suck on that pearl and make them cheeks jiggle girl!"

With that I stormed off to get my nephew...her secret stepson his damn Peanut Butter Crunch!

∞

"Ahhhh shit! Fuck no girl! What the hell are you trying to do?! You know I don't fuck no breeders, so go ahead and drop back down on your knees! Yeah that's right! Sssssssssss!" I scolded Kamisha's simple ass.

I had been fucking with her off and on since before my brother even met her ass. Once she became pregnant with my nephew, it was a wrap for me. Luckily, I had stopped fucking her after finding out my brother was laying that pipe in her, so I knew Jackson wasn't mine. I already knew that she had trapped my brother. She was the scandalous bitch who had inspired me to be consistent about wrapping it up.

My brother was doing the responsible thing by wrapping it up, yet he allowed Kamisha to handle and supply some of the condoms that they'd used. That was a huge mistake. A mistake that he'd be living with for the rest of his life. I know he loved Jackson, but I also know that if he had the opportunity to go back and change things, he would.

I personally didn't fuck with women with kids. I was paranoid that they'd try to trap me. From time to time I allowed Kamisha to give me some neck, but after she swallowed my nut, I always made the bitch guzzle some Pepsi.

I assumed that if Pepsi could be used as a cleanser, then it could destroy my sperm cells as well. If the bitch threw that shit up and my sperm somehow managed to survive and impregnate her conniving ass, then she deserved my baby. That baby would definitely be meant to be, in that case.

After coating Kamisha's esophagus with my liquid gold, I got down to business. I told Kamisha that I would give her broke ass five-thousand dollars if she could manage to seduce and fuck Lyle at least once and provide proof. I told her that if she was able to rekindle their relationship and keep the shit going for a few months then there would be an additional ten-thousand dollars at the end of her ghetto ass rainbow.

As I suspected, her eyes lit up at the prospect of not only having that kind of money, but also at having another chance with my brother. Although, she was the one who informed me that my brother couldn't fuck, I knew that she still loved the hell out of him. I gave her some pointers that I thought would work in her favor. Confident that she was all in, I stood up and zipped up my fly.

Laying twenty-five hundred dollars on her coffee table I said, "Here's an advance to get you started. Clean yourself up a little bit...stop looking so rachet. If you knew what his wife looked like you'd see where I am coming from. Make no mistake, if this shit doesn't work in your favor, you better keep my name out of your mouth. Oh, and if you are unsuccessful, you will pay me back with interest!"

With that, I walked out of her cheap front door counting down the days before I could officially bring Julissa home.

« Chapter 22 Small Favor »

"Lyle"

"SHIT! I'M LATE!!!" I shouted to no one in particular. I couldn't remember if I had set my alarm or not. I heard the water going in the shower and knew my wife was already up preparing for her day. I wasn't going to be able to wash my ass, at least not now. I hopped up and dashed towards our walk-in closet.

My groggy ass tripped over the thick throw rug in our bedroom and I tumbled onto the bench at the foot of our bed. Julissa always kept her purse there so of course it flew onto the floor with its contents flying all over the carpet.

"Damn it!!! I don't have time for this shit!" I huffed.

Bending down, I quickly began gathering all of my wife's

belongings and replacing them into her purse. When I came across a hard-circular disk-like case I felt my jaw tighten. I had dated enough women to know that the case most likely contained birth control pills.

Trying to keep my cool, I tried to tell myself that maybe they were old as hell and that she just hadn't thrown the shit away yet. Just as the thought ran through my mind even, I couldn't make myself believe that.

I popped open the cartridge and sure enough, she had recently filled that prescription. There were five pills missing and she appeared to be caught up on her days. It was Friday and even that pill had been popped from the bubble pack already.

Damn, the first thought that crossed her mind in the morning was not having my baby. Who the hell took a pill as soon as they rolled out of bed?! I was so upset that I didn't even realize that tears were streaming down my face. I was breathing heavily and tempted to strangle my deceitful wife to death. She had played me. Not that I minded, but I had fucked her practically every day of our marriage and was confused as to why I couldn't get her pregnant.

We were a few fucks away from me scheduling a fertility appointment. She saw the impact that not knocking her up had on me. She sat back watching me question myself. I felt like less of a man because I couldn't even get my wife pregnant. Why the fuck didn't she want my seed?! What was wrong with her?

She had just started a war and as she happily sung in the shower...she didn't even know it. If my dear wife wanted to play, I'd be Chucky!

I walked over to my nightstand and took pictures of the birth control case, and name of her specific brand. I placed her birth control pills back into her purse and continued with what

I needed to do. I wanted to be long gone before she got out of the shower. I probably would've killed her ass if I had to look at her right now. I didn't want her to see that I had been crying either. I threw on the first thing that I saw and kept it moving. I could finish getting ready at work in my office.

Being at work that day was tortuous. All I could think about was Julissa and how she'd been deceiving me throughout our entire marriage. I felt as if it had all been a lie. I know I had a secret child out there and very little room to talk but damn...this shit hurt.

What wife wouldn't want her husband's baby?! Of all days, this day in particular was super busy. Normally I had moments when I could leave, but this was not that day. I was so fucked up and distracted that even my brother noticed and called me out on it.

"Yo Lyle! What is up with you today man? The lights are on, but no one is home nigga! Talk to me, does this have anything to do with Julissa?" He asked.

I couldn't help the tears that flew out of my eyes. Honestly, I didn't even care. If I couldn't be vulnerable with my twin, who could I be vulnerable with?

My brother patiently waited as my shoulders shook from me crying so hard. Once I regained my composure, I hoarsely whispered, "My wife has been taking birth control pills."

"Hunh. What?!" He asked dumbfounded.

Clearing my throat, I repeated, "My wife has been taking birth control pills bro. She's been lying to me the entire time. The bitch doesn't want my seed Kyle! You don't know how close I came to killing her ass this morning. How could she do this to me man? I'm not just some random nigga off the street, I'm her fucking husband!"

"Now, I know she doesn't want kids right now, but she could have been honest about those pills. She really had me anxiously waiting each month hoping that she would miss her period. Of course, that shit never happened because the bitch has been taking those God damn pills!!!" My voice boomed.

"Damn, that's some heavy shit right there, bro. I'm sorry this shit is happening to you. What did she say when you confronted her about them? Tell me you didn't do nothing stupid...?" He replied looking worried.

Shaking my head, I said, "Naw man, I'm not like that anymore. I'd never hurt my wife. I cried like I'm doing now and left before anything could happen. She doesn't even know that I know about them."

Before I met my wife, I did have a minor problem with my temper and keeping my hands to myself, but thanks to some counseling and anger management classes, I've been doing just fine. I'd never hurt my wife.

"So, what are you going to do?" Kyle asked.

Shrugging my shoulders, I said, "There's really nothing I can do man. I guess I will just have to wait until she is ready. I'm tired of fighting with her about the same damn thing. Until she decides she wants a baby, I'll have to be satisfied with Jackson for now. At least I have him."

My brother simply threw his hands up in defeat. I had just fed him a load of shit. I planned on doing plenty, but I wasn't about to tell his ass that. He already thought I was crazy. Once he left my office, I put my plan in motion.

∞

I sent my cousin Amaria who happened to be a Pharmacist a text message.

Me: Hey cuzzo.

Thirty-seven minutes later...

Amaria: Hey big head! What's up?!

Me: A lot, but it's too much to text. Look, I need a small favor.

Amaria: Oh Lord, what is it this time? You didn't get burned again did you?

Me: Hell no girl! You know I'm married now!

Amaria: And that means...???

Me: I've never cheated on my wife.

Amaria: Okay, okay. Congratulations again. What's the favor then?

Me: I'm going to send you a couple of pictures. Let me know when you receive them.

Five minutes later...

Amaria: Got them. Why are you sending me pictures of Ortho Tri-Cyclen?

Me: I need you to give me a few prescriptions of this, only instead of actual birth control pills put sugar pills in there that look similar. My wife's information is in the pics. Make it look just like that please! My wife is sharp and notices everything.

Amaria: Lyle, this is wrong cousin. I don't know all of

the details and don't need to in order to see that this is fucked up.

Me: Amaria, cut the shit! Since when did you become all high and mighty? Did you forget who took care of your stepdaddy problems. Better yet, did you forget who helped pay for those fancy degrees?

Amaria: Fine! You're lucky you're my favorite cousin! The shit will be ready in an hour now leave me alone I'm at work!

Me: I love you too and thanks!!!

I couldn't get off of work fast enough so that I could pick up my wife's placebo. I met my cousin with a brand-new Gucci bag that I snagged on my way over to see her. That woman loved purses more than anyone I had ever met.

It was my peace offering. I knew I was about to do some fuck boy shit, but Julissa had already done some fuck girl shit to me first. She started this mess, but I was sure as shit going to finish it.

When I gave Amaria the purse she jumped up and down and acted like a fool in there. That was one of the reasons why she was my favorite cousin. No matter how successful she became, she remained humble and grounded. Sure, she could afford her own bags, but she still showed her appreciation as if she didn't rake in six figures each year.

She showed me the pills and I was shocked at how well she had done. Of course, I needed to pop out the first five pills before swapping out the prescriptions, but aside from that, there were no differences. My cousin was a lifesaver.

"Thank you so much for doing this Amaria. I know that you don't agree with me on this but trust me, you have just saved my marriage." I told her before kissing her on her forehead and walking out.

∞

It was difficult trying to act normal around my wife knowing what she was up to. I wasted no time swapping out the prescriptions as soon as she busied herself with our supper. I stashed her real prescription deep inside of my briefcase. I would dispose of it tomorrow.

Next, I needed Julissa to have a moderately severe accident that wouldn't kill her, but would potentially get her disqualified from the military. She was getting out whether she liked it or not! I could take care of her and she knew it.

You don't have to tell me; I already know that I am one screwed up individual. You'd have to be in my shoes to fully understand why I made the decisions that I did. It was because of the love that I had for my wife. I wanted to preserve our marriage. I just couldn't think of any ways to hurt her that weren't too drastic.

The answer to my problems came to me in my sleep. I had a few people who owed me some favors. It was time for me to tap into those favors.

« Chapter 23 Facetime »

"Julissa"

I KNEW LYLE WAS GOING to be mad about me having to work this weekend, but it was beyond my control. Our one-year anniversary was the upcoming Saturday and I was on the schedule for twelve hours. I didn't even know how to break the news to him. I was on the military's time and they essentially owned me as well as my time.

If they ordered me to work sixty days straight, then that is what needed to be done. I knew he didn't understand that concept nor was he trying to understand. I loved my husband, but I loved the Air Force, too. Asking me to choose between the two was like asking me to choose between my atria and my ventricles. I couldn't survive without either of them.

Tonight, I was going to have to lay it on thick. I'd make one of his favorite dishes and end the night with another one of his boring ass sex sessions. We could always celebrate our anniversary early, couldn't we? Either way, my hands were tied, and I would be on base serving my country.

While we already had a freezer full of food, I knew that I wouldn't have time to defrost anything. I'd have to stop by the grocery store before I made it home. My husband loved my famous Mississippi pot roast, with sweet corn, potatoes and corn bread. I hoped a full belly was able to chill him out just a little bit.

I stopped by a nearby Walmart Supercenter and hoped that it wasn't too packed. I wanted to get in and out so that I could beat Lyle home. Typically, I parked super far from my destinations in order to get my steps in on my Fitbit, but today I parked in the expectant mother's spot. Kiss my ass, I was on a mission!

I found a small cart and darted into the store. Upon entering the store, I made a beeline to the food section. As usual, I picked up everything that crossed my path. I could never go into that damn store without spending unnecessary money. By the time I finished weaving in and out of the countless aisles, I know I had at least three hundred dollars' worth of food in my cart.

"I should've eaten before I came here." I mumbled to myself.

Of course, the checkout lines were packed. I walked the width of the store in search of the line that was the shortest. As I reached the aisle next to the end, I spotted Amethyst ringing out the customers in her line. Her line was just as long as the rest, so I figured I'd just get in her line. I wanted to invite her on an Alaskan cruise that me and Lyle were thinking about going on next month anyway. It was on my bucket list and I hoped that she was able to get the time off.

My girl was in her zone and didn't even notice me until I was the second person in line. When she spotted me, her eyes got big and a look of shame was plastered across her face. I don't know why she'd feel that way in front of me.

I was her biggest cheerleader and I was proud of the changes that she was making to become an independent woman. She was the MVP as far as I was concerned. Hell, I was happier for her now more than I had ever been.

It was finally my turn and I was beaming with pride looking at my bestie. She sported her best resting bitch face and looked as if being at work was the very last place on Earth that she wanted to be.

"Hey heifer! I forgot that you worked at this Walmart. I'm so proud of you sis!" I genuinely gushed.

"Yeah, well this place is nothing to be proud of. I feel like such a loser. I'm embarrassed every time I put on this uniform. I bet the groceries in your shopping cart total out to be worth more than my whole paycheck." She replied sadly.

"Amy, you need to stop. Be grateful that you even have a job to come to. A lot of people aren't able. Consider this a steppingstone that will eventually lead to where you want to go. Some people would kill to be in your shoes. Trust me, it could be so much worse."

"I suppose you're right. I know I should be grateful. It's just hard watching everyone around me prosper while I remain in this rut."

"You were stagnant before. But, now you are making major moves. Trust me, you got it going on, love. You have your own crib, car, you're in school, and you have a job. You are winning!!! Anyway, Lyle and I are going on an Alaskan Cruise next month and I wanted to know if you and Kyle wanted to come. I'm sorry for the short notice, but we just decided to go last week. See if you can get off!"

"Damn that sounds like fun. I could really use a vacation from this job! This past month has been kicking my ass! Hopefully my manager will approve it if I tell her it was a preemployment vacation and I will check with Kyle. His ass is going to have to pay because my pockets are deflated as fuck!" She joked.

"Well I'm crossing my fingers because it won't be the same without you there." I pouted.

The customer behind me cleared her throat hinting around for us to hurry the hell up. I apologized to her, paid my four hundred- and eight-dollar bill and threatened my bestie to keep me posted about the trip.

I was so behind schedule with cooking for my man. I sped home and immediately started my meal. I normally liked to put the roast in the crockpot, but today I had to improvise. I didn't have that kind of time. Earlier in the week I had purchased him a gold Rolex watch for our anniversary.

I was going to present it to him today. I had seen him admiring it for some time now and I had been saving up for it. I wanted to use my own money to get Lyle his present. I wasn't much of a watch fan, but I have to admit, it was nice as hell. I couldn't wait to see his face light up.

While our supper cooked, I took the liberty of taking a quick shower to wash the day away. Once I got out and applied my body butter, I couldn't help but to notice that it was way past time for my husband to be home. Not wanting to be *that* wife, I continued on with setting the tone for the evening.

I learned from my last romantic gesture to just keep things simple. The night that I took my Aunt Kandi's advice turned into one of the most humiliating nights ever. I felt horrible for Lyle. His dick was crunchy for two days! He had to stay home because the hives were too itchy for him to attempt to work. Maybe we were destined for a boring sex life. It shouldn't be too bad since I didn't know any other way.

Once our food was done, I set the table. I kept the food on the warmer and waited patiently for my husband to come home. An hour passed, followed by two more. I had finally broken down and sent him a couple of text messages, but they went unread and unanswered. By the time midnight had rolled around, I had called my husband a whopping five times.

My voice messages went from concern to rage. I was so livid and seeing red that it took two glasses of wine for me to calm down enough to think to call Kyle. He should know where my husband was since they worked together. He could have at least called. The worst images went through my mind as I pictured him dead in a ditch. Where on Earth could he be?

"Hello, Kyle?" I asked unsure if he had answered because it was so quiet on the other line.

"Yes, Lissa? Is everything okay?" He asked groggily.

I felt terrible for waking him up. I know he had to be up super early because Lyle was always up at the crack of dawn.

"Yes, it's me. Lyle hasn't been home. Have you seen him?"

"Uhhhhhh...as a matter of fact, he did mention wanting to stake out a couple of our properties. We have been having some of the strangest things happening and we want to see if we can catch the fuckers. I will stake them out tomorrow." He replied.

Clutching my chest, I sighed in relief.

"He still could've called me and told me that. He had me worried sick thinking his ass was in the bottom of Crystal Lake. I'm going to kill him when I see his ass!" I cried.

I was an emotional wreck. I was relieved, yet still pissed off that he didn't make a simple phone call. I continued to cry into the phone as Kyle attentively listened.

After a few minutes I pulled myself together and apologized for waking Kyle up with me and Lyle's drama.

"Nonsense. I'm glad to help and will always be here for

you Lissa. If I were your man, you'd never be up late at night wondering about my whereabouts. I'd never make you cry. Why can't you see that baby? Do you want me to come over there until he comes home?"

I shook my head as if he could see me through the phone. "No...no that isn't necessary."

"Are you sure? You know I don't mind keeping you company, love."

"No, I'll be okay now that I know that he's safe. I have to get up early in the morning for work."

"Lissa?"

"What K?"

"What are you wearing?" He asked.

"That's none of your business perv."

"Come on Lissa. Tell me, what are you wearing baby?"

"I should be going now K..." I trailed.

Just then I noticed that he was beckoning me to accept his video call. I was frozen in panic. What was I to do?!

Against my better judgement, I closed my eyes as I hit the 'answer' button. I suppose curiosity got the best of me.

It took a moment for our images to focus and I melted at how good he looked even fresh out of his sleep.

"Damn you are so fucking gorgeous!" His voice caressed my ear.

"What are we doing Kyle? We can't keep doing this."

"What are we doing? As far as I'm concerned, we are just two good friends chatting. What's the harm in that?"

"You know why K. I'm married to your..."

"And as I told you before, fuck him." He cut me off.

I was silent as I thought about how wrong what we were doing felt. I was furious at my husband, but I still shouldn't be doing what it was that I was doing.

"I want you Julissa. I want to taste you. I know my brother isn't hitting that pussy right. I can give you multiple orgasms baby. Give me a shot."

"Kyle I'm going to hang up if you keep this shit up. It just isn't right."

"Okay then. Can we just pleasure one another over the phone? Let me see your titties."

"No! I'm not showing you shit."

"Why not Lissa? Don't be afraid. No one will ever have to know what we are doing right now. It stays between me and you."

"I'll even kickstart it." He continued.

He then pulled back his comforter exposing his over-sized meaty dick. I didn't know that they were capable of being so large. My mouth dropped open as I felt my lady parts down below begin to stir. I looked on lustfully as he began to stroke himself and moan. As hard as I tried to pry my eyes away from the screen, I was in a trance.

"Come on Lissa. I want you to cum with me sweetheart."

I shook my head.

"Please baby. Pull those panties down and play with that fat cat." He moaned.

I don't know what it was about that last statement, but I lost all my inhibitions. I felt as if he had dickmatized me. I was in a trance as I felt my panties sliding down over my plump ass. My eyes lowered as I became aroused.

Pulling my shirt and bra off, I heard him gasp at the sight of my nudity. I laid back onto my marital bed and played with my erect nipples. I licked and sucked on them as he watched me. All the while he was still going to town on his third leg.

"Let me see *her* Lissa." He requested referring to my coochie.

I licked two of my fingers and seductively placed them on my budding pearl.

"Shit girl! Mmmmmm play with that pussy." He growled.

"Ummmmm Kyle! This feels sooooo good!!!" I bellowed.

He and I shared in the most intimate moment that I had experienced up to that point. It was so vivid that I could almost feel him touching me through the phone. We timed our climaxes perfectly together and I felt an immediate closeness from what we had just shared.

My husband had never brought me to such heights when we were together, so I knew he was incapable of such a feat via Facetime. We eventually ended our call in the wee hours of the morning, and I drifted off to a peaceful sleep with little regard to my husband or his whereabouts.

« Chapter 24 Neither Here Nor There »

"Amethyst"

I WAS HAVING A ROUGH day up until I saw Julissa, then it went further into hell from there. Don't get me wrong, I loved my bestie, but sometimes seeing her reminded me of everything I wasn't. I nearly shit on myself when I noticed her in my checkout line. I have known her long enough to know that when she had told me that she was proud of me that she was being truthful, but for some reason I still felt like a failure.

It had always been that way. She had always been an overachiever. She had always been a straight A student, while I studied my ass off for my C averages. Academics came natural to her. You'd think since I grew up in a two-parent household that I would've had the brighter future between the two of us. Although I was extremely proud of my girl, I just wished that I was able to experience some of the successes and satisfaction that she had in her life.

She had a great career, one that was noble and offered a retirement plan after twenty years of service. That heifer could literally retire by the time she was thirty-eight, if she wanted to! She was a female pilot! How bad ass was that?

Most people can't even say that they personally even knew a pilot. She hadn't pursued furthering her education either; however, the resources were there should she decide to. I knew she was interested in engineering. But why would she want to since she was already a pilot?

She was also happily married to a handsome, successful black man. She was living the life that I should have. I had put in more time and work with Kyle than she had with Lyle. I know she complained about their sex life, but in my opinion that was a minor technicality. They could work together and fix that issue. I wish that bad sex was me and Kyle's biggest issue. Hell, good sex seemed to be the only thing we had going for one another these days.

Although we were still a couple, I felt him slipping further and further away from me. I wasn't sure if there was a remedy for our problems. I was doing everything humanly possible to make us okay again, but sometimes I feared it was too late. It was strange not being able to just pop up over Kyle's house anymore. I missed having a key to his place. Today I had called him after I got off work, but he had told me that he was exhausted and wasn't up for company.

I had pretty much begged him to come over because I hated sleeping alone, but he just wouldn't budge. All I wanted to do was be in his presence, I wouldn't have disturbed his rest. After being rejected, I was in a somber mood as I drove home.

I bet Julissa never had to beg Lyle to come over prior to them getting married. Hell, it was probably Lyle's weak ass begging her to come over to spend time with him. Why couldn't Kyle's heart soften a little more towards me?

Once I pulled into the front of my house, I sucked my teeth at the sight of Denzel sitting on the steps that led to my door. For a second, I thought about speeding off, but then I realized that I had nowhere to go.

My supposed man had already told me that I couldn't come over to his place. My best friend had plans for her wedding anniversary with her hubby and I didn't want to impose. My mom's house was filthy and I couldn't afford a hotel room for the night.

Turning the engine off, I sat and stared at Denzel. His fluffy ass was staring right back at me. I wasn't sure why he was at my house. I had made it crystal clear that what we had was over. Denzel wasn't a bad looking man at all. In fact, he had a very handsome face. Very nice features, but I preferred my men chocolate. Plus, he was about five foot eight inches tall and was pushing three hundred and fifty pounds.

Denzel was a little on the freaky side. While he had no attraction to men, whatsoever, he thoroughly enjoyed ass play and being dominated. We had spent countless hours fucking one another silly.

He had a nice sized stick, but his large belly sometimes made it difficult for him to perform to my satisfaction. He tended to get winded fairly easily too. Sometimes sucking on his chest freaked me out because it felt like I was sucking on lady tits due to their ginormous size.

Since I couldn't remain in my vehicle for forever, I eventually opened my car door and reluctantly made my way over to Denzel. As I got closer, I heard him say, "Damn baby, I thought that I was going to have to go over there and get you. Don't you miss me?"

"Denzel, what we had was good and I am appreciative for all that you have done for me over the years, but it's over now. I told you this already. Things are getting more serious between my man and I want to give him my undivided attention."

"I don't want to creep around on him behind his back anymore. He deserves that much." I said trying to be as honest, yet as considerate as I could be with my choice of words.

"I've tried to respect your relationship and your wishes, but after being away for a couple of months, I have missed you. I didn't realize it until you cut me off that I love you Amy. I'm not asking for a lot, just a little bit of your time every now and then. I won't wear out my welcome. I just want to love you for the time that we are together. Don't cut me off completely though...I need you Amy." He pleaded.

His humility tugged at my heartstrings and I couldn't help

but to feel a certain level of compassion for Denzel. I didn't love him, not even in the slightest, but he reminded me of how I sometimes had to begged for Kyle's love and attention. I hated that feeling and just didn't have the heart to make him feel the way I often felt.

Walking past him and up to my front door, I turned and said, "Okay Denzel, but no more pop ups. I don't want to risk Kyle or my nosy ass neighbors seeing you. Oh yeah, and the price has gone up."

He sported a big Kool-Aid smile as he replied, "Well, that's inflation for you baby."

∞

Before I had gone to work, I had taken out a package of ground beef. I wasn't much of a cook; however, I could make one hell of a bacon cheeseburger and fries. As I busied myself in the kitchen. Denzel was stretched out on my couch like a beach whale.

I busted out laughing at the thought of asking him to buy me a new one because he had left a permanent indentation in it. It would make for an awkward conversation, but I knew my ass was crazy enough to do it.

After adding the finishing touches to our burgers and fries, I carried them into the living room. I then went back and grabbed us a couple of sodas from the fridge. Living on a budget had me eating out less and cooking more.

Lately I had been a huge fan of Pinterest. It was certainly helping me with my culinary woes. Denzel complimented me several times about how seasoned and juicy his burger was. I thanked him and smiled.

Once our plates were bare, I felt him rubbing on my thigh. I rolled my eyes because I really wasn't in the mood for sex, but I did enjoy having his company. I wanted to just sit and have an adult conversation. I knew that he and I would end up fucking, because that was what we did. He had never just come over to just talk.

"Ummmm, Denzel, let me jump into the shower. I still have my work clothes on."

"I don't care about that shit. You could never stink or be dirty in my eyes. Hell, it would be nice to see what that cat is like in its natural state. My timing is perfect too, if my memory serves me correctly, you should've gotten off of your period three days ago. Am I correct?" He cockily asked.

I took a moment to think about his statement. I didn't recall having a period a week ago. In fact, I really couldn't recall the last time that I had had one. For a lack of words to say, I replied with a fake smile plastered on my face, "You sure know me well Denzel."

He and I spent the next hour sexing one another. I always enjoyed using a strap on him because it afforded me the opportunity to release my built-up frustrations. I ordered his fat ass around and inflicted pain just the way he liked it.

I made him crawl around and submit to my every demand. I fucked Denzel until his asshole was wide enough for me to see high up into his intestines, stomach, esophagus, and out through his mouth. Ordinarily, I would allow him to stick around for cuddles...but not tonight.

In light of my absent period, I needed to take a pregnancy test to confirm or deny my suspicions. I hadn't even noticed any changes going on with my body. I hadn't been nauseas, my breasts weren't tender, and I wasn't craving ice, pickles, or dirt.

I felt like my normal self. I had been pregnant years earlier and there was no mistaking that shit. I was miserable for the entire two months leading up to my abortion. I didn't want it, but my mother made me have the procedure done.

After sending Denzel home to his wife and kids, I walked into my bathroom. I already had several pregnancy tests from my prior pregnancy scares. I checked their expiration dates and they were all still good.

I had to calm myself down as the magnitude of my situation sank in. I knew that if I were pregnant, it damn sure wasn't my boyfriend's baby. He kept his nut locked up tighter than a virgin's pussy. Denzel on the other hand loved to cream-pie me every chance he got.

I used to take the morning after pill, but since it happened so often, I had become lazy. I wasn't on birth control because I was holding on to hope that my man would one day knock me up. Now as I stared down at the three positive pregnancy tests sitting on my bathroom counter, I knew I was royally fucked, but that was neither here nor there.

« Chapter 25 That Old Thing »

"Julissa"

WHEN I WOKE UP THE morning after Kyle and I had phone sex, I realized that my husband's side of the bed was still unoccupied. Rolling over, I retrieved my phone off of my nightstand. I became annoyed all over again after realizing that he still hadn't bothered to call or text me.

Well two could play that game. Sadly, it was officially our first anniversary and it was already starting off terribly. It was bad enough that I had to work the day of and after, but to add insult to injury my husband had forgotten where he lived and how his cellphone operated.

I found a legal pad and a pen and simply wrote, *'Working this weekend.'*

I then left it on his nightstand.

I knew eventually he'd crawl out of whatever hole he was in, and when he did, I would not be answering for his ass just as he had done to me. I put my phone in Do Not Disturb mode and set off to getting ready for the long weekend ahead of me.

At the end of my shift, I was going to stay the night with Olivia and my dad, so I packed some extra clothes. I was certainly in a petty mood. I was going to let him wonder about me tonight.

I was dragging from my late-night rendezvous with my brother-in-law, so I knew that I'd definitely be stopping by Dunkin' Donuts for an Iced Macchiato to pick me up. I took a long, warm shower hoping that it would wash my exhaustion and troubles away. Once I was satisfied that my body was clean, I stepped out of our massive his and her shower.

After drying off, I applied my French vanilla scented body butter. I always took pride in my appearance, but since it was my anniversary, I wanted to look a little extra special. At least as much as I could while still adhering to the Air Force's dress code policy.

I had learned a lot of neat makeup tricks from my best friend over the years. Even though I wasn't a huge makeup person, I always thought it was gorgeous. Today I was going to beat my face.

I took my time ensuring that I steadied my hand as I expertly worked on my face. Once I was finished, I couldn't stop staring at my own reflection. Given the limited time, there wasn't much time to devote to my long mane.

I opted to put it up in a sleek low bun and ensured that my edges were on fleeky fleek. Lastly, I put on the uniform that was just brought from the cleaners. I was looking like a whole entire snack in my uniform.

Glancing at the time on my Fitbit, I realized that I needed to get going if I was going to make it to Dunkin' Donuts. Walking out of my house with my work and overnight bags, I was disappointed that my husband and his car were still MIA. I quickly pushed thoughts of him aside because I was determined to have a great day with or without him. Getting into my car, I pulled off anxious to get my favorite iced drink.

"Oh damn!" I shouted in frustration as I noticed the long line wrapped around the restaurant.

There was no way that I would make it to work in time if I waited in the drive-thru line. Then I looked through the windows of the building and noticed that their line inside was not long at all.

"Screw it." I told myself as I pulled into a nearby parking space. I speed walked because I wanted to beat the other people who had the same idea as I did.

While standing in line, I was frozen in place when an all too familiar voice was heard behind me. Trying not to be detected I held my breath as if that would do something and I remained as still as I could considering I was in plain sight.

I was a damn fool for believing that I could hide with my attention-grabbing uniform on. Being nosy, I realized that it sounded as if he were conversing with a woman. As predicted, the line moved fairly quickly and soon I was next up in line.

"Good morning, welcome to Dunkin' Donuts. How may I help you?" The woman at the register pleasantly asked.

"Good morning. I'll just take an Iced Macchiato to go please."

"Sure thing. Coming right up ma'am."

I hadn't even taken my wallet out of my work bag before I felt a hand touch my elbow. I closed my eyes tightly as I braced for an unwelcomed reunion. After silently counting to five, I reopened my eyes and slowly turned around.

"Wow! I thought that was you Julissa. You look incredible!" He beamed bringing me in for a warm hug.

I remained stiff as a board. I was never one for fake pleasantries. Once he released me from his grasp, I dryly replied, "Hello to you, too, Xavier."

His female companion quickly reminded him that she was standing there by obnoxiously clearing her throat. He then tore his eyes from me and looked over at the basic chick standing next to him.

Quickly sizing her up, I was confident that she was no threat at all. Xavier was a very handsome man and could have done much much better. The woman was white and was on the geeky side. She had short mousy brown hair and dark brown eyes that were covered by thick bifocal glasses.

Freckles were plastered all over her pale thin face. Her thin pink lips were nearly nonexistent. She was taller than me, but then again, most people were. She appeared to be anorexic and there were no curves in sight.

Yeah, my first love could've done much better than the fuckery standing before me. Home girl needed a meal or ten, but I was in no position to judge her or anyone else. I didn't know her and wasn't interested in getting to know her. If he liked it, I loved it.

Xavier's senses finally kicked in and he decided to introduce me to his female companion.

"Julissa, this is my girlfriend, Brooklyn. Brooklyn, this is Julissa. I've told you about her."

Brooklyn felt it necessary to clear her dry ass throat again. I was tempted to reach into my work bag and give her raggedy ass a cough drop to loosen up those secretions.

"I'm actually his fiancée." She proudly boasted showcasing a nearly invisible engagement ring.

Ignoring her insecure ass gesture, I rebutted, "Cute ring Brooklyn! Well, congratulations to the both of you! Today is actually *my* one-year wedding anniversary."

With that, I flashed them both my massive rock. They both appeared to be taken aback by its blinding beauty...for different reasons of course.

Brooklyn seemed to ease up a little bit after hearing that I was married.

"That sure is some ring, Julissa. Happy first anniversary!" Brooklyn exclaimed.

"Wait, you're married?" Xavier asked still stuck on stupid.

"Yes, I am married. *Happily* married.' I responded emphasizing how happy we were.

My husband was currently on my shit list, but they didn't need to know that. Up until last night, I *was* happy.

By that time, I was being called up to get my drink and they still had yet to order. I needed to get my ass to work.

After getting my drink I replied, "Well, Xavier, it was nice seeing you again and Brooklyn it was a pleasure to meet you. Congrats again on your upcoming nuptials."

Brooklyn bid me a speedy farewell while Xavier was standing there looking butt hurt. His eyes hadn't left me once. I was now happy that I had taken the extra time to get ready this morning. I knew that even in my uniform, I was looking fierce!

I made it to work in the nick of time. It was fairly uneventful aside for my husband blowing my phone up every second of the day. I only knew that because I had briefly taken the Do Not Disturb feature off of my phone just in case. Plus, there was no satisfaction in ignoring my husband if I didn't even know when he called or texted.

His texts messages and calls started out as apologetic and sweet, but once he found my note about me working this weekend especially on our anniversary, he became unglued. He told me that I needed to come home now and that I needed to consider a different career path because he wasn't going to allow me to disrupt our family. While I found some of his bullshit funny, I didn't think that anything that he said about the military was humorous.

I allowed his bullshit for a little while longer before just blocking his ass. Why should I ignore the world when it was only my husband that I didn't want to speak to?"

I had asked my superiors to prevent him from coming into my work area that weekend should he attempt to stop by. At the conclusion of my day, I happily skipped out of there and was prepared to make the forty-minute commute to my parents' house.

I was hungry and had decided that I would stop by a Wendy's on my way there. I had called and asked my parents if they wanted something from Wendy's and of course they both told me yes.

Olivia had started dialysis and knew that she wasn't supposed to be eating fast food, so she just asked for a salad and a chocolate frosty. My dad on the other hand ordered damn near everything on the left side of the menu.

After grabbing our food, I was reminiscing to Jill Scott's beautiful ballad, 'He Loves Me'. I loved that damn song! It was so beautifully written and arranged. The love that she sang about was what dreams were made of. I collaborated with Jill by assisting her with the completion of her song:

You're different and special

You're different and special in every way imaginable

You love me from my hair follicles to my toenails

You got me feeling like the breeze, easy and free and lovely and new

Oh when you touch me I just can't control it

When you touch me...

I belted when I felt something slam into the rear of my car. My heart started beating out of my chest when I realized that I was no longer in control of my vehicle. I had never been in a car accident before and I considered myself to be a fairly decent defensive driver. I tried to slam on my brakes, but they were ineffective. I really lost it and panicked then. I turned the steering wheel wildly in one last ditch effort to regain control.

It was all in vain because I soon spotted a large tree in my path and I quickly plowed into it.

« Chapter 26 Isn't It Ironic »

"Lyle"

"HELLO, MAY I SPEAK to Mr. Carlton please?"

"This is him speaking. Who is this?" I asked already knowing.

"Hi Mr. Carlton, my name is Angela and I am an ER nurse here at Beth Israel Deaconess Medical Center. Sir, I am contacting you because your wife has been in an accident. She is currently in surgery so you should try to make arrangements to get here as soon as you can." She spouted robotically.

"Oh shit! Is she going to be alright?!" I asked.

Although I had planned my wife's attack, I was concerned that her injuries were severe enough to negate surgery. Surgery for what?!

"Unfortunately, I am unable to provide any additional details Mr. Carlton. How soon are you able to make it here?" She asked.

"I can be there in less than thirty minutes. I'm on my way there now!" I told her before disconnecting the call.

My mind was racing all the way over to the hospital. I wondered if somehow the cops knew that I had something to do with her accident and was awaiting my arrival. Was this an ambush? As afraid as I was to go to the hospital, I knew that I couldn't just not show up.

What kind of husband would I be if I didn't check on her well-being? I was genuinely concerned and knew that I had gone too far. I immediately regretted my decision. I called her father, my brother, and Amy and told them everything that the nurse had told me...which wasn't much.

Both Julissa's dad and Amy verbalized their worry and got off the phone. But no, not my arrogant ass nosy brother. I felt as if I were being interrogated by the God damn police. I eventually had to cut him off by hanging up on his ass once I reached the hospital. After rushing inside, I was directed to the waiting area outside of the hospital's operating room.

I had met Angela, the nurse, and she had told me that my wife was still in surgery. She still wasn't offering up any additional details. It pissed me off because I not only needed to know that my wife was okay, but I also needed to know whether or not my plan had worked. I hated to think that I had done it all for nothing.

After pacing for a bit, I sat down and placed my hands over my face as I began to rock back and forth. My mind was racing and I was losing my cool as dozens of "what ifs" circulated through my weary mind. I had told God that if my wife made it through whatever injuries she was afflicted with; I would support her no matter what. I just needed her to be okay.

"Oh no Kyle! There's your brother and he isn't looking too good! Fuck! Lyle is she..." I heard Amy ask unable to finish.

Wiping the tears from my face I replied, "I don't know man. She is still in fucking surgery! Fuck!!!" I shouted punching the chair beside me.

Amy was crying her eyes out, but my brother looked like a raging bull. His jaw was clenched tight and I could tell that he wanted to ask me more questions. I didn't have time to entertain his ass though. Just as Julissa's parents and Aunt Kandi rushed through the double doors, her surgeon appeared from the restricted area.

"Hello, are you the family of Julissa Meyers?" He asked.

"Yes, we are the family of Julissa *Carlton*." I corrected.

I knew it wasn't the time or the place, but fuck that. She was my wife and would be addressed as such. It infuriated me that she still had not taken the proper steps to legally change her surname to mine.

She had told me that she was on it. First the birth control pills and now this shit. One thing was for damn sure, just as soon as her ass was able to sit in a wheelchair; she was changing her last name once and for all!

"Oh, please accept my apology sir. Her driver's license still has her maiden name apparently. Anyhow, I'm Dr. Adkisson and I am the surgeon who performed Julissa's surgery. She was apparently the victim of a hit and run accident. As she was driving, she was rear ended by a secondary vehicle. The other vehicle was driving at an excessively fast speed.

According to the police who responded to the crime scene, she had tried to regain control of her vehicle, however, she struck a tree. Luckily none of her injuries were life threatening individually, however, they were quite extensive collectively.

She suffered a broken nose from the impact of her hitting her face against the steering wheel. She has fractured several ribs, which will resolve on their own in time. Her pelvis suffered the most damage.

She suffered a crush injury to her pelvis that unfortunately, affected some of her reproductive organs such as her left fallopian tube. I tried my best to repair it, however, I was unsuccessful. Even if I had repaired it, she would've most likely ended up with an ectopic pregnancy from the scarring in the future which would've potentially been life threatening for her had it ruptured.

With her now having only one fallopian tube coupled with the general trauma to that area, her chances of conceiving again have been drastically reduced, however, it is still possible. That brings..."

"What the hell do you mean conceive again?" I inquired.

Dr. Adkisson's face softened as he looked at me sympathetically. He then said, "I'm sorry to have to be the one to tell you this Mr. Carlton, but your wife was approximately seven weeks pregnant. The accident put too much stress on her body and she miscarried. She is in the recovery room now.

Give us about thirty minutes to get her moved and you can see her. Try to limit the visitors to two people at a time. I don't want to overwhelm her. I'm not certain if she was aware of her pregnancy or not, but at any rate, she is going to need lots of love right now. Her injuries will heal in time, but the devastation from losing a child can last a lifetime."

Dr. Adkisson spoke with us for a few more minutes prior to excusing himself to go and check on my wife. I didn't hear much else after his old ass had told us that I had basically killed my own baby. I wanted to scream and so I did. I screamed at the top of my lungs because the enormity of what I had done was simply too much to bear.

I was a monster who had gone through a lot of trouble to have my wife injured in order to get her permanently disqualified from the Air Force. I had done it all to jumpstart my little family, yet my family had already been jumpstarted. I just didn't know it. I hadn't noticed any changes with her at all. She was still as active as she had always been. I wondered if she knew and was waiting to surprise me.

I was so devastated. My seed was gone, all because of me. I knew that although my wife was not ready for a family, she wouldn't have ever terminated the pregnancy. She didn't believe in that shit and neither did I. Isn't it ironic how the one thing that I was risking it all to achieve was already in production? I should've left it all in God's hands because he had my back all along.

I continued screaming and eventually I started throwing chairs around in the waiting area. I remember my family trying to calm me down, but I was inconsolable. I vaguely remember the hospital's security team coming in my direction...but I don't recall anything thereafter.

« Chapter 27 What's Going On? »

"Kyle"

I WASN'T EXACTLY SURE what the hell was going on with the muthafuckas around me, but they had me all the way fucked up. Some bullshit was going down, but I just couldn't put my finger on it. Receiving that phone call from my brother about Lissa being in a terrible accident nearly caused me to have a stroke. I gave him the third degree until his ignorant ass hung up on me.

I knew that I needed to calm down a little bit because I was behaving more like Lissa's husband than just her brother-in-law.

Not knowing the full story or whether or not she was

going to be okay was killing me on the way there. I had damn near left Amy behind who was moving just a tad bit too slow for me. When it came to Lissa, I'd leave damn near anyone to check on her well-being.

Once we finally reached the hospital, it took everything in me not to shake the truth out of my brother. I had known him longer than even our parents had, so I knew when he was on bullshit when I saw it. I was fuming when we were told that Julissa was involved in a serious hit and run accident. What kind of monster would do such a thing?

I hated hearing about her injuries. She was in for one hell of a recovery process and I would be there to help her in any way that she needed me. One thing was certain, I was not happy to hear that she was pregnant with my brother's child.

That shit was like a slap to the face. I know that you will think that I'm a terrible person for what I am about to say, but I was overjoyed to hear that she had lost that baby.

That nigga already had a son with one of my former jump off's. He was not about to have a baby with my woman. He had me all the way fucked up. I wondered how she had gotten pregnant in the first place. The last time I checked, he was crying like a little bitch because she was on birth control. Had he forced my baby into getting off of her pills? What was really going on?

My brother had showed his ass so much at the hospital that he had to be subdued and sent to the ER. There were talks of possibly admitting him to psych, but we didn't have time for that shit. We had important business meetings scheduled for the upcoming week and as my partner, he needed to be present.

Seeing Julissa in that hospital bed all swollen and defenseless had me crying on the inside.

I hated that I couldn't love on her the way that I wanted to. Although, my brother had been taken to the emergency room, Amy, Aunt Kandi, and Julissa's parents were still there. I always got vibes that her aunt didn't like me for some reason, but she never said anything out of the way to me.

I wanted to plant tender kisses all over Lissa's face and hands, but I couldn't. I wanted to kick all of their asses out, but I knew that I couldn't. Instead, I sat there and stared at her bandaged face waiting for her to wake up. I needed to see how much she remembered.

I hoped that she came around before my brother was released. Something was fishy about his bitch ass and I honestly didn't trust her alone with him anymore. But again, it wasn't my place to stop him.

We all sat vigil at her bedside, waiting for her to wake up. It took her four long hours to fully rouse. When she did, she told us about how she had just left from picking up food from Wendy's when she was hit from behind. She stated that when she attempted to slow the car down, she noticed that her brake lines had been tampered with or something rendering her unable to slow the car down.

She remembered seeing a tall tree before everything went completely dark. Her next memory was of her waking up with us all at her bedside. Although she was in pain, she was in great spirits. She was shocked upon hearing that she was pregnant since she was religiously taking her birth control pills.

She admitted to us that she had been taking birth control pills and joked that she was going to have a serious talk with her gynecologist once she was better. I knew with the injuries to her pelvis; she wouldn't be intimate with Lyle for some time and I was happy about that.

I was about to pull out all of my tricks to make her mine at last. My brother had failed her. He couldn't protect her the way that I could. Hell, I still had a feeling that he had something to do with all of this mess.

Only time would tell. If I received confirmation that he had anything to do with her being laid up in that damn hospital bed, I was going to forget that he was my brother and murk his ass.

Speaking of brothers, we had discovered that Amy's alcoholic ass brother, Travis was the one sneaking into our properties and damaging shit. That bastard had cost us a grip and I was going to find out what his angle was. I know his ugly ass wasn't still pissed off about being fired.

Sure, he did seamless work *when* he showed up...but who knew when that would be. He was too unreliable for me. I relied on my employees heavily at the work site and everyone had a role. Every time he failed to report to work, his assigned task was put on hold.

Those frequent holds began to chip away at my pockets. Ihad tried to help the little muthafucka out and even offered to pay for him to go to a rehab facility. He wasn't interested because in his little addict mind, he didn't have an issue. He was certain that he could stop drinking whenever he wanted to.

The night that I had told Julissa that Lyle was staking out our properties, he truly was. I had somehow managed to "misplace" my brother's phone without his knowledge. By the time that he noticed, it was too late for him to leave his post. He knew that he was already on my shit list, so he knew better than to leave and possibly risk being detected.

I knew that if she couldn't get a hold of Lyle by a reasonable hour then she would reach out to me. While I had relayed the message about him staking out the house, I failed to mention the *lost* phone. I didn't feel that the specifics were necessary.

My heart smiled when I noticed her calling on the other end. I even altered my voice to make it sound as if I had been asleep. That couldn't be further from the truth. I was wide awake and anxiously waiting for her to call me. I even told Amy that she couldn't come over because I was too tired for company. I wanted to be able to give Lissa my undivided attention and that would be difficult with Amy's clingy ass all up on me.

Our phone sex was everything! The brief glimpses of her bare body did something to me. I would pick having phone sex with Lissa over having physical sex with Amy any day! We connected on such a deep level. I came so hard that night and slept with a smile on my face afterwards.

The next morning, I got up with that same smile spread across my face. I took care of my morning hygiene and left the house to meet my brother. He wasn't in his car which was odd, so I decided to go into the house to investigate. Upon entering the two-story home, I noticed my brother in the living room sitting on the love seat. Loud whimpering caught my attention. It was coming from the direction of the family room.

Walking in that direction, I instantly grew pissed at the sight of Travis's hogtied body lying on the floor. He was almost unrecognizable from the ass whooping my brother had surely blessed him with. I flashed him a sinister smile and proceeded to walk around his battered body several times.

"Hey Lyle, why didn't you wait for me? You took a huge risk apprehending him by yourself...especially without your phone." I scolded.

"Man, fuck him. He was no threat to me at all!" He countered.

"Well Travis, as I'm sure you have figured out, you have royally fucked up. I don't see this ending well for you, however, I suggest you get to talking if you want to spare the ones that you love nigga." I said kicking him hard in the side of his face.

I was grossed out my damn self when I watched his jaw pop out of place.

"Get to talking!" I barked.

« Chapter 28 Kamisha's Web »

"Lyle"

IT HAD BEEN FOUR WEEKS since my wife's accident and I still found it difficult to look her in her eyes. I had never meant to cause her so much pain. I just wanted her to be hurt just enough for the military to not want her. Unfortunately, my plan had backfired in many ways.

I had caused her to lose the very baby that I had plotted so methodically to have. Now I wasn't sure if she'd ever conceive again with the removal of one of her fallopian tubes and the damage to her pelvis. Her car was totaled, so now I was tasked with getting her a new luxury car.

I hadn't purchased the car that she had so I replaced her BMW in the exact color, make and model. The only thing that differed was the year of the car. I upgraded her to a newer model. My wife's recovery was tough, and I found it difficult to even get my wife alone.

Her mom, dad, aunt, best friend, and my brother occupied most of her time. We hadn't really had any private conversations regarding the accident. I suppose there was no need to inquire about what I already knew.

I could've lost my wife that fateful day. I was filled with regret and still couldn't believe that I was willing to risk it all over her career choice. While I was still strongly against it, I now realized that I'd rather have her in the Air Force rather than not at all. Facing the possibility of losing her was a little too close for comfort. She was finally back up on her feet, but was still experiencing a great deal of pain.

The icing on the cake was when I'd discovered that none of her injuries were disqualifying. She was already talking about returning to work and it infuriated me. I told her that she could take it easy and just focus on enrolling in school, but she wasn't hearing any of that.

I was at my wits end and nothing that I had tried seemed to be working. There was so much drama going on around me that I felt as if I was suffocating.

For starters, my brother was being weird about Julissa's accident. Talking to him sometimes felt like talking to the FBI. He was so determined to get to the bottom of who had tampered with her brake lines and caused her accident. He vowed that when he found out their identity that they would pay for what they had done to his sister-in-law. He was acting more like a concerned husband instead of a brother-in-law in my book. I was starting not to trust his ass around my wife.

I know he often teased her and pretended that he couldn't stand her, but I was starting to see beyond that false façade. I was almost certain that my brother wanted my wife and I would kill his ass if he ever tried it. I was growing increasingly paranoid of almost everyone. I guess a lot of it had to do with how I was living.

I had been unfaithful to my wife and that shit was eating me alive. I couldn't believe that I had back peddled and allowed myself to get caught up in Kamisha's sticky web again.

As usual, she had been on some bullshit and holding my son as leverage. For some reason, she wouldn't allow me to take my son over to Kyle's house like I normally did. She was insisting that if I wanted to spend time with Jackson, then it needed to be at her house.

I didn't like the shit, but I just wanted to be with my son, so I complied. My wife was laid up in bed healing and she always had people over there looking after her, so I didn't feel that I'd be missed. I always felt as if I was put on the backburner when it came to my wife. Her career always came first. With Kamisha, I always felt like the most important thing in her life. She made me a priority.

Don't get me wrong, my wife cooked for me every day and sexed me, too, on demand, but she was always so busy otherwise. I could call Kamisha at three in the morning just to talk and she'd listen. Kamisha would jump at the chance to become a stay at home mom, yet I literally had to trap my own wife into getting pregnant.

Spending more time with both Kamisha and Jackson together put a lot of shit into perspective. It all started out innocently enough. I'd come over and Kamisha would greet me at the door looking amazing. She looked different from her usual skimpy attire.

She would always wear classy, yet flirty clothing which was much different from what I was used to with her. She now had that mommy glow up look. Kamisha was a beautiful woman. She always reminded me of a young Dorothy Dandridge...just rachet.

We would always eat our meals together as a family. We would play games with our son and talk about everything under the sun. Kamisha said everything that I needed to hear at that time.

I confided in her about being unhappy about my wife's career choice and about her losing our baby. I was actually vulnerable with her and I cried grown man tears into her bosom.

It was in that moment that I stopped seeing her as just a money-grubbing baby mama, but as a friend. When she straddled my lap, I knew I should've thrown her ass onto the ground and immediately left, but having her undivided attention felt amazing. Plus, she had matured and was so very different.

My conflicted feelings rendered me paralyzed as I felt Kamisha sensually lower her full lips down on top of mine. As our tongues danced together, I could literally feel the heat scorching me from in between her thighs.

"I'm married." I heard myself whisper against her lips.

"I know and that was a mistake baby daddy." She rebutted.

She slid down my body and unzipped my pants. She knew I wasn't into all of that extra foreplay shit. Pulling my fully erect dick out of the opening in my boxers and pants, her eyes grew large.

"Damn baby. Oh, how I've missed him!" She stated seductively removing her sundress. She wore no panties or a bra.

As she stood up to mount my dick, I quickly snatched my erection away from her.

"Naw, I don't have a condom ma." I stated honestly. I hadn't come over there with the intentions of fucking her so of course I was not prepared.

"I got us covered." She said.

"Fuck that! I love Jackson and all, but he is the product of you having us covered the last time." I snapped losing my erection.

Instead of responding, she stood to her feet and walked towards the direction of her bedroom. I continued sitting in the same position with my dick still hanging out. Just as I was about to put him away, Kamisha returned with a sealed box of condoms.

"As you can see, this is a brand-new box of condoms. You can inspect the box and the condoms on the inside. I'm not on no shady shit with you Lyle, baby. I just want us to be a family." She cooed.

I thought about the situation long and hard. I had no business even contemplating doing what I was about to do. I could always pull out with the condom on before I even came to reduce the chances of me impregnating her sneaky ass again.

Although I did not want any more children with her, but with my wife, it wouldn't be the end of the world if I did. Hell, I wasn't even sure if my wife was even capable of giving me any seeds now.

I allowed my little head to take over as I opened up the box of condoms and expertly put one on. I then ordered my son's mom to sit on my dick. It had been well over a month since I had been up inside of some pussy due to my wife's injuries.

She wasn't even scheduled to see her gynecologist to give her the green light to resume sexual activities for another two weeks. I needed what Kamisha was giving me. With every moist stroke, my wife fell further and further from my mind.

That was over a month ago, now essentially every free moment I had was spent over at Kamisha's with her and my son. I was truly living a double life out here.

« Chapter 29 Justice »

"Amethyst"

"MA! SOME DETECTIVES are at the door!" I yelled at my mother from her front door.

"I'm coming!" My mama shouted back.

I stood there eyeballing the two tall, dark, and handsome detectives. I had been coming over to help my mom more often around the house and taking her to her doctor's appointments since my brother Travis had gone MIA.

We weren't really alarmed because he had done this shit in the past. He was perhaps mama's favorite child and they were pretty close, so she personally felt his absence the most.

We assumed that his ass had found a new chick and was laid up under her. That is until those detectives arrived. Once mama finally waddled her big ass to the front door, detectives Tony and Stonebrock had reintroduced themselves to her. We all exchanged informal pleasantries before the pair finally stated their business.

"Well ladies, do you know a man by the name of Travis Jeffries?" Detective Tony inquired.

"That's my son." Mama admitted.

"That's my brother." I whispered solemnly.

We both responded in unison.

Both of their faces took on somber expressions and, in my heart, I knew that I was not going to like what they were about to say.

"What about my son are you inquiring? Has he done something wrong? Is he okay?" Mama asked.

Staring into detective Stonebrock's eyes and reading them, I replied, "No mama. Travis is dead. They've come to tell me that my brother is dead!" My voice cracked.

The room was spinning and I could see my mama's body start to fall. Luckily, detective Tony was able to catch her. I was in shock and barely noticed detective Stonebrock's arms wrapped around my shaky body.

"I am so sorry for your loss ma'am. Go ahead and let it out. We will be here for as long as you and your mother need us to be." Detective Stonebrock stated empathetically.

I did just that. Why would anyone want to kill my brother? He was such a good man even with his alcohol addiction. He was always a self-less person and would give you the shirt off his back. Damn, I couldn't believe that he was gone. I was going to miss his voice, smile, and his goofy ass sense of humor.

"What happened?" I finally asked in a hoarse voice.

"We are still trying to figure that out. What we do know is that he was beaten badly and that his fingers were all removed. We aren't sure if the killer was attempting to hide his identity or to pass on a message. In my personal experience, if the killer was trying to mask your brother's identity, they would've also pulled his teeth or removed his head altogether. That makes identification extremely difficult.

With that being said, his body was dumped in the back of a liquor store. It does not appear that he was killed right away due to the various bruises covering his body. While some were fresh, others were days old. Due to the severe beatings he sustained, we would like for a family member to come down to the coroner's office to identify the body."

I started crying again at the thought of the hell my brother had endured. It sounded as if he had suffered for at least a week before he died. No one deserved that shit.

"I can't see my brother like that! I can't!" I screamed.

"Actually, there are a couple of tattoos on the victim. Maybe you can describe them to us for identification." Detective Tony chimed in while holding my hysterical mother's hands.

"Travis had three tattoos that I know of. He has a tattoo of praying hands on the right side of his chest. He has a portrait of the singer, Aaliyah, on his mid-back, and the last tattoo is our mother's name and date of birth on his neck."

"It was actually that last tattoo that brought us to you. We assumed that it was someone special to the victim; otherwise their name would not be permanently inked on his body. Thankfully JaQuel Jeffries is an unusual name so we found you all right away." Detective Stonebrock added.

"You have given a perfect description of the victim's tattoos. I am comfortable with considering this as good as a positive identification. Here's our business cards so please do not hesitate to contact us should you have any questions. I assure you that we will do everything in our power to find out who killed your brother and your son."

The detectives promised to keep in touch before heading off to deliver someone else's family life altering news.

Glancing at my mama, I hugged her and promised that no matter what, we would get justice for Travis.

« Chapter 30 Pillow Talk »

"Julissa"

"JULISSA MEYERS...JULISSA Meyers..."

"I'm over here." I replied standing up and walking over towards the medical assistant.

I handed her the clip board which held the documents that I'd been asked to complete.

"How are you today?" She asked.

"I'm blessed. How about you?"

"It's Friday so I cannot complain Ms. Meyers."

"Oh, please just call me Julissa or Lissa for short." I requested, not correcting her for calling me Ms. instead of Mrs.

"No problem. My name is Fantasia. Right this way Lissa."

I trailed behind Fantasia who brought me to a scale. She took my weight and height. I provided a urine sample as well. She then led me to an unoccupied room and obtained my vital signs.

She asked me a variety of questions based on my answers from the documents I had filled out. She gave me a paper vest and a paper sheet to cover up with and told me that the doctor would be in soon. She then retreated from the room, giving me privacy to change.

Less than five minutes later, Dr. Li entered the small room. She was a young Asian OB-GYN that I had been coming to since I started getting my biennial checkups.

"Hi Julissa. How are you feeling girlie?" Dr. Li asked.

"I am doing so much better than I was. I've just been given the okay to return back to work, but I need you to clear me to resume making love to my husband. He's about to leave me if I don't put out soon." I half joked.

Lately, there had been some changes in Lyle. He was extremely secretive and distracted. He was coming home sometimes later than usual, but was unable to account for his time. I had a nagging suspicion that he was fooling around on me.

The very thought of my husband being with another woman shattered my heart into pieces. It also made me question my job as a wife and as a woman. Up until my accident, there was never a time when I had denied him in the bedroom. I even tried to spice shit up. Was I not enough for him?

Of course, like anyone else would do I asked him about his whereabouts and inquired as to whether or not he was cheating on me. Of course, his response was always the same. He would deny having an affair and told me that I was crazy for even suggesting it. He assured me that I was more than enough woman for him and that he'd never stepped out on our marriage.

As badly as I wanted to believe him, it was extremely difficult to at times. Maybe I was insecure because I hadn't been able to perform my wifely duties as I always did. Maybe once Dr. Li cleared me and I was able to throw this good cootie cat at him, things would go back to the way they were.

Thank goodness for my family and friends because my husband was rarely home anymore especially on the weekends. Deep down, I was starting the think that he blamed me for the miscarriage and was avoiding me. I felt my husband slipping away and I didn't know if it was too late to catch him.

Don't judge me, but Xavier had reached out to me almost immediately after my accident. News of my hit and run accident had traveled around our town and reached him. He had begged to see me in the hospital, but I was no dummy and told him that wouldn't be a good idea. Our conversations were innocent for the most part...at least on my end.

Sometimes I found myself having to remind him that I was married and that he had a fiancé. He often expressed regret over the way things ended between the two of us. I'd always reiterate how things happened for a reason even if we didn't fully understand those reasons.

He told me that he had met Brooklyn through a mutual friend and that they'd been together for a little over a year. I shared with him how I met my husband, too. Xavier showered me with attention and made me laugh during the dark moments when I felt gloomy. Kyle was there a lot too, but I knew that he was wearing down my barriers and I tried to limit our alone time to a minimum.

I hadn't told Lyle yet, but I was returning to work the upcoming Monday. I knew that was going to cause a pow wow of its own.

"It looks like your bleeding and cramping has completely subsided according to your paperwork. Do you feel ready to resume having sex?" Dr. Li asked pulling me from my thoughts.

"I actually do, Dr. Li. I'm beyond ready now that the bleeding has stopped."

"That's great to hear. Can I take a quick peek?" Dr. Li asked.

"Sure, it isn't like you haven't seen my va jay jay a million and one times before." I shrugged with my legs cocked wide open in the stirrups.

We both laughed.

As Dr. Li assessed my lady parts, I thought about my marriage and remembered to inquire about an alternative birth control pill since the last one had obviously failed me. I had tried the IUD in the past, but I kept getting infections from it. That shit had me walking around smelling like mackerel. The shots made me bleed for months on end and I didn't want the Nexplanon because of the ugly scarring so my only option was a stronger pill at the moment.

After she told me that everything looked great down below, she cleared me for sex. I then requested that she prescribed me an alternative pill which she gladly did. I guess my body had become immune to the last one after years of usage. Dr. Li told me that I was free to get redressed and that she would call in my new script to the pharmacy.

As I was exiting my room, I noticed a woman who looked just like Amy walking into a room adjacent from my own. What the hell was Amy doing here? I wondered. Instead of barging into her room like the nosy bitch buried inside of me told me to do, I shot her a quick text.

Me: Hey heifer, what are you up to?

A few minutes later once I reached my car she had texted back.

Amethyst: Nothing much. I'm just taking a little nap before work this evening.

I couldn't believe that she had just outright lied to me like that!

Me: Damn, I was going to ask you to come hang out for manis and pedis. Get some rest boo and hit me up when you get a minute.

Amethyst: Will do. TTYL.

I stood in front of her car enraged by her boldfaced lie. She could've just told me that she was at the OB-GYN, but didn't want to discuss the matter any further. I would've respected her privacy. But, the lie, I just couldn't handle.

I looked around and dedicated the next couple of minutes to slashing all four of her raggedy ass tires. The wires were showing any damn way. I knew her ass wouldn't call me for help since she had just lied and told me that she was in bed.

I knew she was grieving and all for her bullshit ass brother, but fuck his nasty ass. I cannot tell you how many times I would wake up to him feeling on me and shit while I was asleep at their house growing up. I was like the only person her mother would allow over since the house was always so dirty.

Then he always insisted that I be his wife whenever we played house. No matter what the scenario was, it always led to the wife and husband dry humping. I hated those games. I hated him even more.

Even as an adult he would cop feels here and there until I finally snapped one of his fingers. He finally learned to keep it moving when he saw me. I didn't even want to attend that fucker's funeral but since she was my family, I had to support her through one of her darkest moments.

Satisfied with my handiwork, I quickly got into my new car and sped off in the direction of my home. If there was one thing that I despised, that was a liar. Right now, Amethyst was a liar.

Later that evening I couldn't wait to make love to my husband. Being close to him again was the most euphoric feeling in the world. It was brief, but it was certainly fulfilling. We were both afraid of overdoing it since we were just getting back into the swing of things. He was so attentive to my needs. It was such a great evening that I had accidentally revealed that I was returning to work as we pillow talked.

Lyle opened his mouth as if he were about to say something, yet instead he simply rolled over and ignored me for the remainder of the night.

« Chapter 31 Game Time »

"Kyle"

"**LISTEN KAMISHA, THIS** is what you need to do and it has to happen today. The sooner we pull this shit off, the sooner I'll get my woman and you will have your money." I commanded.

"Damn Kyle, this shit feels so wrong. I do actually love Lyle and I don't want to hurt him. I don't feel right about this K." Kamisha stated.

"Bitch, I'm not paying you to feel, I'm paying you to make some shit happen so that I can get my girl!" I fumed.

I was sick of sitting on the sidelines watching my brother play house with my wife. He still hadn't even manned up and told Lissa about Jackson. Worst of all, he was now banging Kamisha again. I know what your judgmental ass is thinking. While it is true that I set him up and was paying Kamisha to seduce him, he should have been man enough to turn down her advances. If I had Lissa to come home to every night, I'd never even contemplate fucking around with another bitch.

Out of patience, I was going to set it up for my brother to get caught with Kamisha and Jackson today. That little nigga looked just like us, so I knew no introductions would be needed. Lissa was sharp and would catch on to the scene quickly.

"Here's what you're gonna do. Since the two of you have been hanging out really tough, Lissa has already been noticing the changes in his behavior and availability. She's been calling and texting me more often regarding his whereabouts. Lately, instead of covering up for him like I usually do, I simply tell her that I don't know where he is.

I have this burner phone that I am going to text Lissa with. I'm going to pretend to be a person who knows that Lyle is cheating and exactly where to find him. Then I'm going to send her your address." I spoke giving her the plans for the evening.

I would be staking out her house the entire time in a rental car. I told her to make sure that Jackson was playing in the living room while the two of them were in the bedroom knocking boots. Kamisha was also instructed to make sure that she left the front door unlocked. That way Lissa would have no issues entering the home.

I became frustrated at the sour ass look on Kamisha's face, so I roughly squeezed her cheeks until she looked like a bug-eyed fish.

"Bitch, you better not fuck this shit up for me tonight! Wipe that ugly ass look off your face and get ready for game time!" I growled.

"Okay, okay!" She replied swatting my hand away from her reddened face.

"Good. Now that we have that understood, give me a sample of what you are not about to give to my brother's scary ass." I remarked laughing.

With tears in her eyes, Kamisha slowly dropped to her knees and engulfed my meat in one swift motion. I found it cute that she was clearly in love with my brother and that she actually thought that she stood a chance with him. By them both playing house, both of their emotions were all over the place. Their delusional ass judgements were way off.

After Kamisha finished swallowing your boy up, I went to my barber and had him get my shit tight. My dreads were already freshly twisted, so no worries there. I was certain that Lissa would come running right into my welcoming arms after finding out about my brother's affair and secret child. That boy was making my job so easy.

After I left the barbershop, I went and picked up something for me to grub on.

By the time I finished putting something in my stomach, it was game time.

I took a long shower all the while I planned out me and Lissa's future together. She could leave all of her old shit at Lyle's crib. He could donate that shit to Kamisha for all I gave a damn. I would buy my future wife all new shit. Once I got out of the shower, I dried off and sent Lissa the first text of the evening from the burner phone.

Me: Is this Julissa?

She surprisingly texted back right away.

Julissa: Who is this?

Me: A friend of a friend. Now, is this Julissa?

Julissa: I'm not verifying or denying shit until you tell me who the fuck you are first. You texted my muthafucking phone, so you better identify yourself or find yourself blocked!

Panic quickly set in, because I didn't have a secondary burner phone in the event that she decided to block me. I decided that it was time to cut to the chase and get down to business before she blocked my black ass.

Me: My name is Jonise and I am a friend of your husband's girlfriend, Kamisha. I know where Kamisha lives, and I can send you her address so that you can check shit out for yourself. Lyle is over there as we speak. From what I hear, you seem like a nice woman and I cannot sit back and watch my friend destroy another happy family.

After I sent that text, I became nervous that she had blocked me for a minute because she didn't respond back to me for at least ten minutes.

Julissa: Send me Kamisha's address.

That was all she said to me when she finally texted back. I wanted to say so much more to her, but she wasn't with the shit that night. I sent her Kamisha's address and didn't hear another peep out of her after that. I decided to rush over to Kamisha's house so that I'd have front row seats to the drama that I was certain was about to unfold.

When I pulled up, I did not see Lissa's car yet, however I noticed Lyle's car parked behind Kamisha's in her driveway. I parked across the street in my rental car and used glasses and a hoodie to help mask my identity.

I turned on the car's TV and inserted the movie Friday into the DVD player. I could watch that classic a million times and it would never get old. I texted Kamisha and let her know that Lissa was on her way and that I was already parked outside.

She simply responded with the thumb's up emoji.

I was kicked back and laughing hysterically at Smokey's crazy ass taking a shit in the bushes when my baby pulled up. She barely allowed the car to come to a complete stop before she hopped out and quickly ran up the steps. She didn't bother knocking or ringing the doorbell. It was as if she knew that the door would be unlocked for her.

Once she entered the house, I lowered the windows of the car and sat up attentively. I hoped like hell that shit didn't get too bad as I heard loud screaming and yelling coming from inside. I really didn't want to have to blow my cover.

Just as I was about to get out to investigate the loud crashing of glass, a crying Lissa came darting out of the door. As she hightailed it to her candy apple red BMW, my brother's naked ass came barreling after her. Her little ass made it to her car before he could reach her.

For some odd reason his dumb ass thought that it would be a good idea to stand in front of her car after witnessing what she had just seen. I heard him yelling for her to roll down the window and talk to him.

After watching her motion for him to get the hell out of her way several times, my jaw dropped when Lissa hit the gas pedal and I watched as my brother's naked body flew into the air and rolled over the top of her car.

His goofy ass looked as if he was doing a stunt for an action movie only that shit was real life. He landed on the pavement quite hard and wasn't moving. The shit was so comical that I probably would've been dying of laughter if I wasn't so afraid that he was dead out there. All of a sudden, I heard him moaning and then he yelled for Kamisha to take him to the hospital. Her scary ass had been standing in the doorway the entire time.

"Hurry up! I think my fucking arm is broken! That bitch just tried to kill me!" I heard him yelling as I drove by.

"That nigga will live. I'm about to go and get my woman once and for all." I said out loud to no one in particular.

To Be Continued

Do No Harm: License To Kill

Is Coming soon!!!

Inevitable Deceptions: A Heart's Journey To Nowhere 3

Is Coming soon!!!

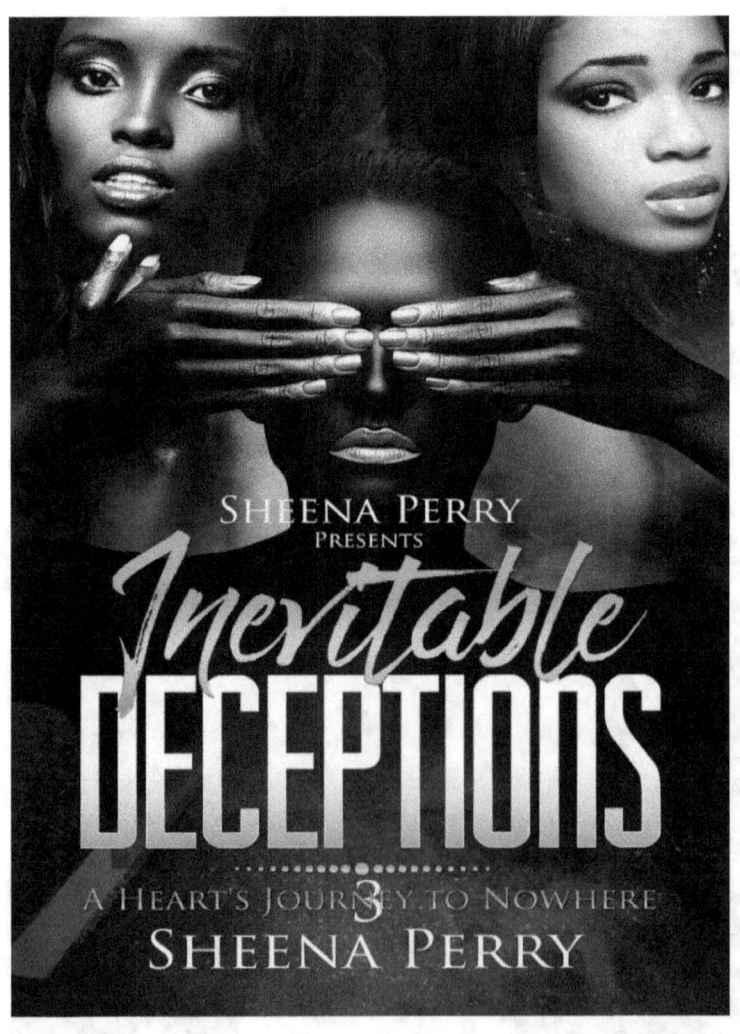

My Brother's Lady, My Baby 2

Available Now!!!

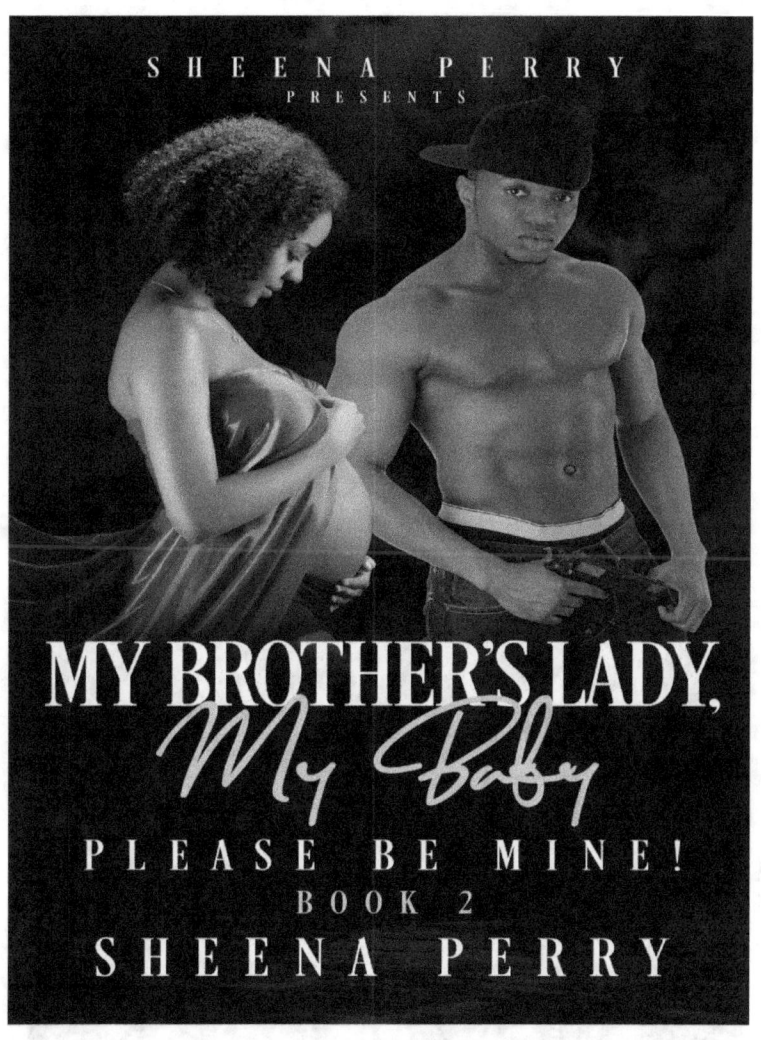

Inevitable Deceptions: A Heart's Journey to Nowhere 1

Available Now!!!

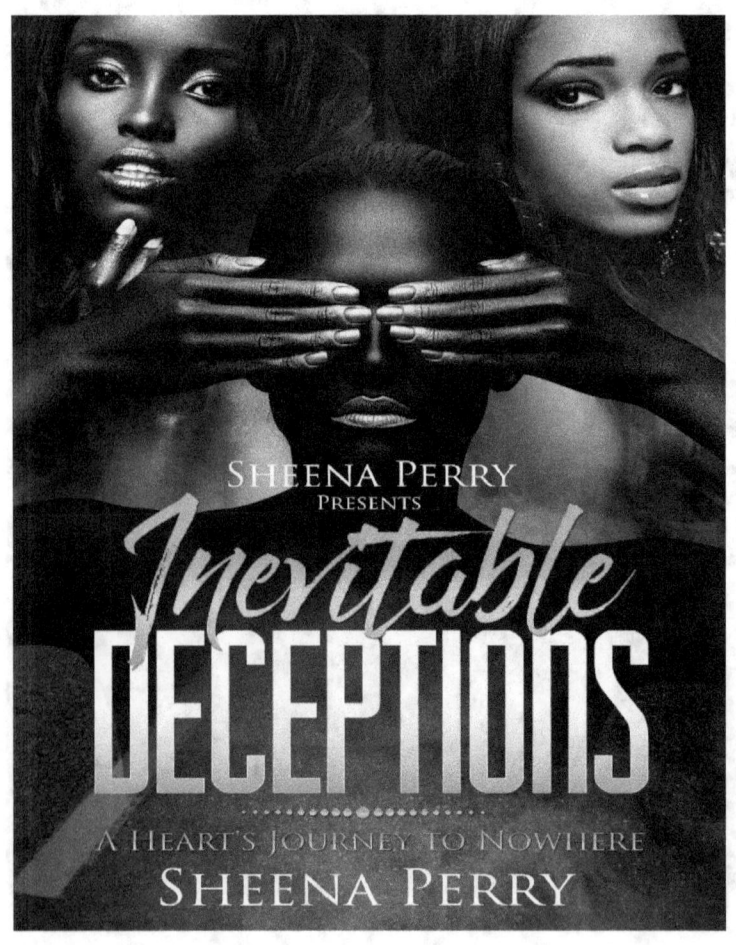

Inevitable Deceptions: A Heart's Journey to Nowhere 2

Available Now!!!

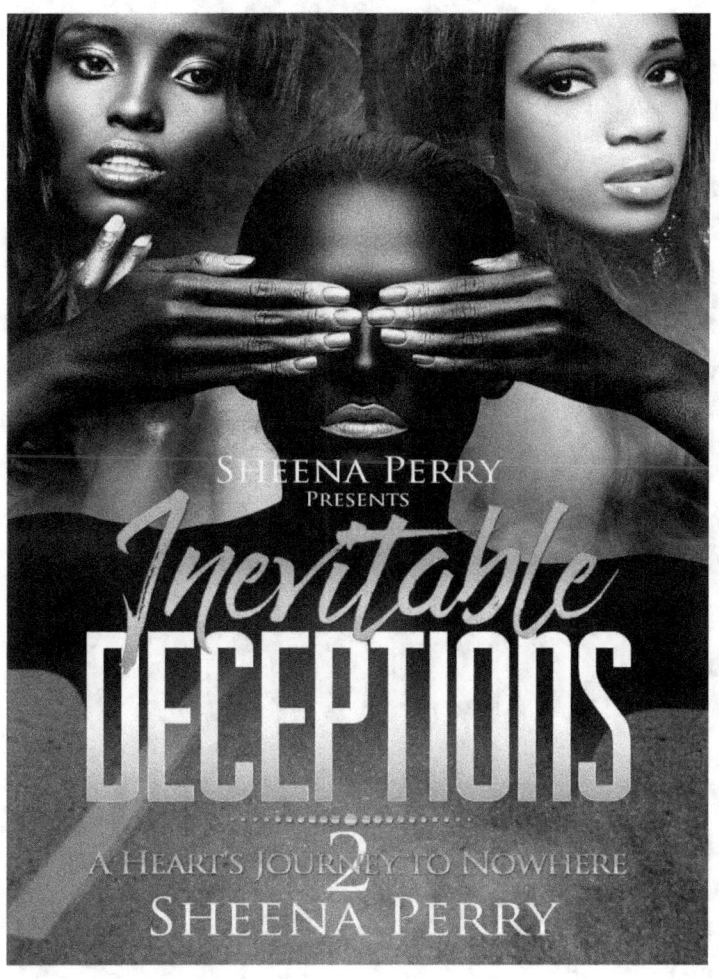

My Wife's Daughters

Available Now!!!

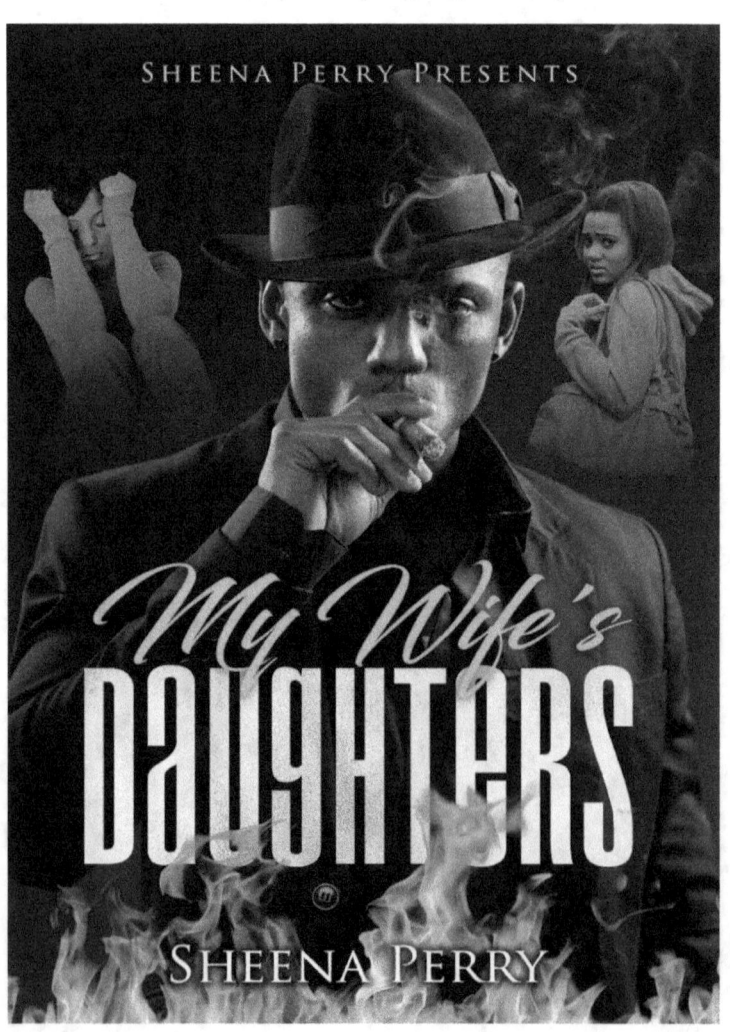

They Call Me Junior: A Gay Love Story

Available Now!!!

They Call Me Junior: A Gay Love Story

Available Now!!!

Releases From Other Authors

Available Now!!!

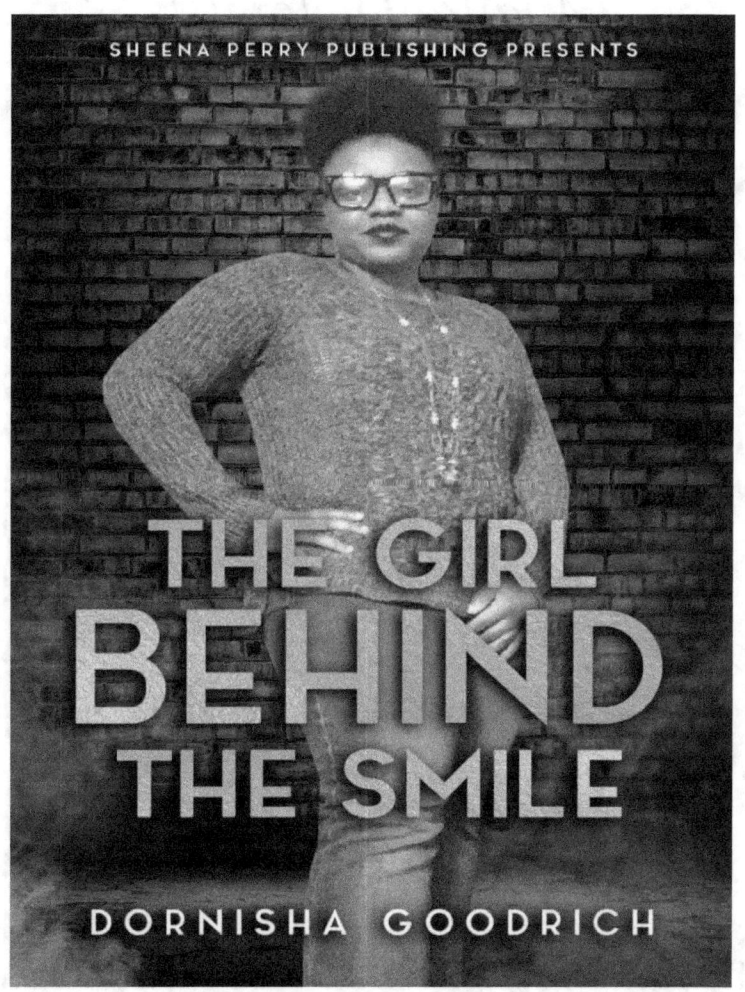

Releases From Other Authors

Available Now!!!

Releases From Other Authors

Available Now!!!

Releases From Other Authors

Is Coming soon!!!

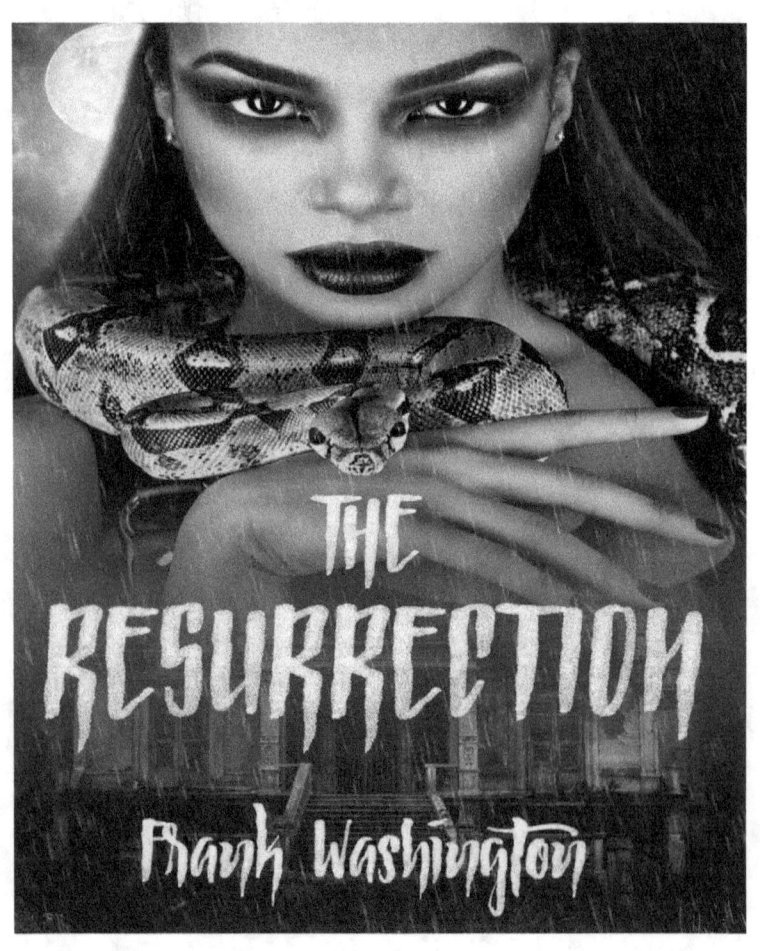